Martha J Wright

The New Garden of Eden

Martha J Wright

The New Garden of Eden

ISBN/EAN: 9783742812490

Manufactured in Europe, USA, Canada, Australia, Japa

Cover: Foto ©Andreas Hilbeck / pixelio.de

Manufactured and distributed by brebook publishing software
(www.brebook.com)

Martha J Wright

The New Garden of Eden

THE

NEW GARDEN OF EDEN:

T.

BAN

San Francisco,

INTRODUCTION.

The poet, Byron, has truthfully said that "Words are things; and a small drop of ink, falling like dew upon a thought, produces that which makes thousands, perhaps millions, think." To be self-taught is to be wise, for investigation reveals, many times, a new light on an old subject quite astonishing to the seeker for truth. Civilization will progress much faster when reason is cultivated and respected as it should be. The presence of the diviner may be known when we allow, kindly, another the same right to think as ourselves.

AUTHOR.

CONTENTS.

CONTENTS.

PART SECOND.

" *The woman's cause is man's; they rise or sink*
Together, dwarfed or godlike, bond or free."
—TENNYSON.

THE
NEW GARDEN OF EDEN.

CHAPTER I.

God in Eden.

God walked amid the ferny bowers;
Entombed was earth with beauteous flowers.
He viewed the mountain, plain and wood;
With rapture said : "My work is good !
A man I'll make this sunny day,
From out this wondrous pile of clay."
A genii in some lofty tree
Sang out that "Life's a mystery.
Then why make Adam from the sand
When you wrought continents most grand
From nothing ? How about a void,
When matter cannot be destroyed ?"

CHAPTER II.

Adam.

The "Garden of Eden" was really quite pretty—
A home for his man in this wonderful city.
God pondered gravely o'er his ideal man,
And thought of results he would now like to scan;
Therefore, as the artist when greatly inspired,
Grasps the pencil ere the vision's retired,
Being quite enchanted with his blissful dream,
Would no longer delay his gódly scheme.
Then the statue of earth he dried in the sun,
Breathed in his nostrils, and Adam was done !

CHAPTER III.

Evolution.

As Adam walked 'round, astonished at seeing
That a life so strange should jump into being
So quickly, so real at one immense bound,
No wonder he was lost in meshes profound,
Of a bewildering sense of life " in the bud,
Metamorphosed from black, sticky mud.
In quite a short time this same Mr. Adam,
Was quite lonely without a dear madam.
The hypnotic sleep no doubt made him weak,
For God gashed his side and a rib he did seek.
By this operation with scalpel or knife,
The rib was secured to make Adam's new wife!
He soon completed our dear mother Eve.
And one more event ere God took his leave:
He waked Mr. Adam from his lethargic state,
And brought him to Eve to see his new mate.
Apollo he seemed by the manifest grace
Of a natural man, with no evil to trace
On his well-formed brow—his beauty to mar,
Nor sin leave its effects like a physical sca r.
At first glance he gave he was greatly amazed,
And he stood transfixed as on her he gazed—
She like an angel so pure from within.
Her spotless soul, without a shadow of sin,
Could plainly be seen by the light of this morn,
'Twas an opaline glow of Beauty just born.
God gave to this pair their first introduction,
And proud was he of his mortal production.
Said he unto Adam, " This is your dear wife;"
To Eve, he explained, her true mate during life.
Adam then kissed his fair Eve on her brow,
And bride she became by the seal of this vow.
The bevy of birds in Nature's grand choir
Sang sweet songs like the notes of the lyre

When softly touched by the god of the muses,
And harmonious sounds all Nature diffuses.
The acme of life had thus been attained,
The summit of wisdom so suddenly gained
In the way of creating a pair divine
In the realm of being in the mortal line.
The acme of life is the heavenly strain,
The summit of wisdom, the gladsome refrain
Of gods of the air as they whisper along
The mountains of joy with this burden of song.
And Orpheus seemed never to tire,
Nature rejoiced by the touch of his lyre.
Memnons arose from the magical plain
And echoed this anthem again and again,
That life of the man and life of the woman,
Crowns earthly existence in thus being human.
The portals in heaven were all left ajar,
And tidings spread quickly to the uttermost star,
Till the universe rang with "Song of the Spheres,"
And the chime will be heard through the incoming years.

CHAPTER IV.

Eve.

It was refreshing in Eden at morn—
No dew-drop reflecting a shadow of scorn;
Nature so lovely in her mantle of flowers,
While Eve walked gaily 'mong Eden's fair bowers,
Quite unconscious of the multitude graces
Centered in self as the mother of races.
She gathered the flowers from the tree and the vine,
And branches also from the cypress and pine.
"The beautiful cypress" an emblem shall be
Through ages to come of immortality.
Again, she exclaimed, the tall, graceful pine,
For the reason 'tis so exceedingly fine,

In future its symbol shall ever be known
As a type of the soul where e'er it is grown.
Eve found another shade of the green,
As pretty a color as any I ween,
It is myrtle she inadvertently said,
And with it she crowned her beautiful head.
She then was as pretty as pretty could be,
A veritable Venus " sprung up from the Sea."
Around our fair Eve was a gleaming parterre,
From lowliest shrub to symmetrical fir.
'Twas a mirror in which sweet Fancy could trace
Such forms as these in Beauty's embrace—
The grotto, the altar, statue and fountain;
The terrace arose, a miniature mountain,
All glowing with flowers arrayed in full bloom,
A vista in which was the sweetest perfume.
Eve now was enchanted with Nature's boudoir.
"Ever be kind" was a voice heard from afar,
Which came like music from some distant clime,
But told not its meaning at this happy time.
She gave the flowers she held in her hand
A kiss of delight, for some fairy-like wand
Passed o'er them, and revealed to her view,
The love of our Father and Mother—God, too.
Nature speaks volumes of love in her eyes,
Through all of her forms and in whatever guise
She may be arrayed, whether sunshine or shower,
In the starry midnight or morn's early hour,
Whether in rock, in the mountain or bird,
The songster's sweet voice or when thunder is heard
To peal forth in tones in lofty disdain
Of the mountain's high crest, or valley and plain.
Eve's joy was like the Sebago's lone lake,
Where never was known e'en a ripple to break
The mirror of waters—so deep in her heart
There nestled a dove, which a peace did impart.
She presently took from her splendid bouquet

A lotus, a pink one, and wondered the way
In which it was clothed; she did greatly admire
The work of the Artist, and then would aspire
To know more of the soul and sense of all things—
A vast source of joy which true knowledge e'er brings.

CHAPTER V.

Eve Explores the Garden.

Eve had been preparing the evening repast.
In the glow of the sunset a glory was cast
O'er her features, and by its reflection
No shadow yet seen by the closest inspection
A heart full of pleasure, whose joy was replete ;
And soon Adam would come for something to eat.
Eve was rewarded, for Adam was seen
Coming to dine with this radiant queen:
The table was built of the rose and the vine,
The daisies, marmosa, and white columbine.
She had prepared in her own dainty way
The figs that she found on that singular day ;
Pomegranates, also, on the table were spread,
So tempting were they with their color so red.
This paradise feast was truly ornate,
For all kinds of fruit graced every plate,
Save one, the apple, which was left on the tree;
For knowledge, as ordered, was never to be
For Adam and Eve.   So then Eve to him said:
" I took a long walk, and somehow was led
To the prettiest spot in this garden to me,
Direct to the home of the fine apple-tree.
Interest increased, as I gave a long look,
'Twas like reading lines from a beautiful book;
Every leaf tremulous, and letters of gold
Shone from each leaflet with a power untold.
' Knowledge is power,' and this tree will bequeath

To the children of earth the green, fadeless wreath
Of knowledge and wisdom, of power and love;
This is my mission in this Edenly grove.
I fain would rest in its delectable shade,
But still roamed onward in a wonderful glade,
And soon I came to a very high fence—
The gate being locked, I could not stray hence.
I saw many strange things—such fishes and frogs,
From graceful beasts to the ugliest hogs.
The cranes jumped around, were trying to dance,
Some horses would neigh, while others would prance;
Strangest of all were the monkeys' grimaces
As I watched their wizened-up faces.
Wish you had been there, for the oddest of all
Was their cute baby, and, indeed, it was small—
That would walk around, just like all the rest,
Turn a somersault oft with baby-like zest.
The mother, so proud of its feats of success,
Would kiss her young babe with a mother's caress;
But beasts of the field came so near to the gate,
Jumping and roaring, each one with its mate
That I gladly came home.   Please, what did you do,
Ere it was my fortune to live here with you?"
Adam's reply was: "For a part of the day
The beasts of the field in one grand array,
Passed by the garden on the fine esplanade,
And names were given while on this parade.
How fine these creatures appeared to the sight,
Not one showing the least sign for a fight!
The lion, the panther, the pig and the bear,
From elephant down to the little gray hare,
All had to be given some kind of a name,
So that we could know what to call all our game."
So Eve concluded not to be frightened,
Confidence gained, her bliss was much heightened;
She called his attention to luminous skies,
As a painting transcendent in glittering dyes,

The crowning effect of a day of delight,
Then dropped at that moment the curtain of night.

CHAPTER VI.

Dove.

As Eve sat watching the lily-white dove,
That was cooing beside her in accents of love,
While its fond caresses were dear to her heart,
She knew not how soon from her pet she must part.
A bright sylvan fairy in cadence sang low
A song of sorrow, from the full depths of woe—
'Twas the sweetest music that Eve had ever heard
From melody imparted by any Eden bird.
The dove for a moment to the woodland had flown.
Dearer and dearer to her heart it had grown;
But soon it returned, and she wanted to kiss
Her dear pet, but lo! there was something amiss,
'Twas lifeless and cold, and a feeling of dread
Came o'er her in horror, for Birdie was dead!
Where the life, the beauty, the glance of the eye?
What was the meaning, or what caused it to die?

Was it a wonder, many ages ago,
Man in his surprise very gladly would know
The great mystery attending life's stern decree,
As in all of its forms find Deity ?
The face of God he can see everywhere,
From tiny insect, to the beast in its lair.
He bowed in reverence to his god in the sun,
For 'twas the home of the glorified One.
In this our own day, though possessed with much pride
For deep erudition that spreads far and wide,
We find all conditions and stages of mind—
The Bushman, the lowest in the scale of mankind,
To the Caucasian's proud entry in fields of renown,

Where glisten immortal the seeds he has sown,
In aiding the progress of man on his way
From savage midnight to the sunlight of day.

———

CHAPTER VII.

A Surprise.

As Eve was gazing on the blissful beyond,
Saw many pictures of which she was fond,
She said to Adam: '' See the landscape's expanse,
Fresh, new beauties await every glance;
See, over there is a falling cascade,
That sparkles in sunlight and never will fade.
It comes from the mountains, so lofty and grand,
Then gracefully falls to the bright, silvery sand;
See how the mountain is kissed by the sky.
It may be God's home,'' she expressed with a sigh.

Just then such a lively commotion arose
In the trees, that Eve said, '' What do you suppose
Such a great twitter among all of the birds
Can mean, that sounds like babel of words?''
The beasts of the field lent their pro rata of noise,
A million times worse than so many school-boys.
The leaves of the trees in a quiver were blown,
Flashes of light came from places unknown
By some magic power which made them exert
All their senses in being alert,
To try to divine the causes that led
The beasts and the birds to be in joy or in dread;
They could not tell which, so in waiting events,
They stood quite in awe of great Nature's intents.
The noise of the beasts now began to subside—
Were thereby transfixed as though stupefied ;
The '' Tree of Life '' flashed like the radiant sun,
And the song-birds chanted their orison.

Something was seen in the sky overhead,
By Adam and Eve, with emotions of dread.
Was it Phœbus, the great orb of day
Wishing to give his respects in that way ?
Or was it Orion away from his throne,
Hurling his darts in bold search of a bone
For his hound?   Such as this great poacher of space
Might seek for his game in the whole human race.
Perhaps it was Taurus escaped from his cage,
Stamping mid-heaven in anger and rage.
Still onward it came, with lightning-like speed,
Direct toward the earth from skyland indeed,
And at last it rested near Adam and Eve,
And, lo ! it was God, who stepped forth to receive
The twain from his electrical car,
Propelled by will power which shone like a star !
Here Adam and Eve, with exceeding great joy,
As well pleased as a child with a fine new toy,
Greeted their Father with an unfeigned delight,
At once more beholding this Father of Might.
God was well pleased with the work they had done,
Commandments obeyed as he told them, each one.
Eve asked her Father if he lived in the sun,
Or on some mountain when the day-course has run!
"I'll tell you, my children," the Father replied,
That I did for ages o'er nothing preside;
Had no companions in the eons long gone,
'Till I 'woke and said that something must be done;
From nought made the earth with all its living host,
Created the starry heavens along the astral coast
Of th' Eternal Sea, that never has an end,
So vast are the realms o'er this ocean's mighty trend.
You can't believe, my children, how much I had to do
Ere I fanned ' the breath of life ' into both of you;
Way up in the heavens I rested for awhile;
Now I've come to see you to be greeted by your smile.
Many thanks, my children; how happy you must be

For all the fruits and flowers that are growing here for ye !"
"Yes," said Eve, "'tis an Eden, but ere I am aware
I'm building constantly fine castles in the air.
It may be wrong, but the truth to you I'll tell:
The restless thoughts that come to me I often try to quell.
'Tis vain; they surge along the empire of my soul;
Like a mighty sea in angry waves they roll;
'Till life; becomes like a dreamy state profound;
And looking into space for some sweeter sound,
To play an instrument with a single key,
Unlocks no arcana of life's mystery.
My dear Father, indeed, while I may be wrong,
In vain I close my ears to this merry song.
To know more of being—of life in every sense—
Is the key I wish to carry all the ages hence.
I realize there's something in the far beyond
That beckons me come forward, never to despond."
A glorious nimbus light encircled her fair brow;
Beautiful she appeared the Father did allow.
The secret of his feelings the sequel soon will show.
He wished not his children in any way to know
The importance of his aim which he first had planned,
Ere Adam's brow was by the Eden breezes fanned.

The music of the birds was in a moment hushed
When the thought he gave to trail her in the dust.
At least the soul-germs of her nature to aspire,
To quench this henceforth by cremation's cruel fire;
Forever she must be as a statue white and cold,
Or a lady on canvas, a beauty to behold.
This was her fortune—as a legacy from God,
And much would be preferred to the carrying of the hod
By one of Nature's noblemen that can understand
Ways and Means of life in the economy of our land.
Light upon the "Tree of Life" began to fade and wane;
The beasts roared in discord all o'er the earthly plain;
The sun veiled in darkness cast a gloomy shade
O'er all the earthland—over all things God had made.

CHAPTER VIII.

The Dream.

The eclipse was momentary—the sun resumed his sway,
The noisy beasts were silent, but in a different way
From God's advent; but were loth to keep
From speaking in a thunder tone, " Darkness thou shalt
    reap;
Ignorance is the harvest, if such seeds are sown
That will yield no wisdom, and knowledge is unknown
By your children." So the cattle reasoned well
As they wandered through the woodland o'er mountain,
    glen and dell.

Eve, lost in reverie, glances o'er the ground,
And delighted with the onyx that she found:
Another rock was pretty, in color gold and white,
While the quartz shone brightly by its inherent light.
The golden coin, say many, is the bane of modern pelf;
Man does not realize it is the self
That's wrong: let the angel of his being quell
The monster Evil in life's chaparral;
Persecution has painted gold quite black,
Yet is ever ready to fill the empty sack
With the shining metal, which will ever rise
A benefactor in the realm of enterprise.
God sat beside her, and Adam, too, was there—
A triad for the time, this God and lovely pair.
Eve in a strange although a thoughtful tone
Said, " Father, in a dream, I traveled all alone
To another country o'er amethystine hills,
And as I this relate, my very being thrills
With emotion impossible to describe.
How lovely were the scenes no artist could transcribe
Their beauty, transported within a jasper wall,
And minarets and towers were so very tall,
The brightness was more dazzling than our sun,

And all their golden streets were fine to look upon.
I met a man who said that he would be my guide,
To see the wonders of this city broad and wide.
So in we went.   'This is the Capitol,' he said;
And 'twas so grand I began to dread
To enter the portal, it was so very fine;
I was so happy, for I saw a face like thine !
But it was so dreary, to see you all alone,
Sitting there on such a beauteous, golden throne
With no goddess by your side with whom you may share
The wealth of your kingdom, or the authors compare
Was told in the mighty flood of years,
Souls be wafted to your kingdom by their fears.
Their great reward was, that fear would make them do
The task of playing on their harps and ever praising you !

Then my guide left me outside the pearly gate.
I floated onward to another heavenly state;
Was enraptured with the suburbs of this town.
Every villa was white as eider-down.
The music from the towers in the skies,
Their chimes was holy as from Paradise.
By magic I entered all their halls,
Saw paintings upon their jeweled walls.
The statues like marble pure and white,
Perfect in loveliness, like human beings quite;
Trees in their gardens were eolian in sound;
Delicious, the airy waves that were wafted all around.
The perfume of the flowers was as incense given
In this land which one might call a heaven.
Then I saw in these supernal homes
Many goddesses within the temple domes
On equal terms with the gods of Upper Air,
Climbing forever progression's golden stair.
They were busy in the line of doing good,
With their documents to see whate'er they could
To ameliorate the causes that underlie the sin

Of frail mortals in the earthland's fearful din.
This was told me, but I did not understand,
Still the waves of harmony striking chords most grand
On the fibers of my heart till I became another being,
By the ambient beauty of this most wondrous seeing."

CHAPTER IX.

Eden Birds.

At that moment the birds came flitting around
In the greatest profusion all over the ground.
The dream for awhile was severed in twain,
For seeing the birds was a pleasure again;
The parrots climbed by the aid of the beak
To the tops of the trees—'twas a singular freak,
And Morea birds with their coating of blue
Were lovely, indeed, in this delicate hue;
The throat and the tail were so changed in the light,
To a brown or gold that was charming and bright;
They chase the prince-orioles, whose fairy-like track
Was known by the hue of orange and black.

The impeyan pheasant with its raiment of green,
The tints alternating its metallical sheen,
With bronze-steel-blue and the violet, told
Its right appellation is " bird of gold."

The humming-bird, flying with its light and flame—
" Kissing Flower," indeed, is a suitable name—
Always enjoys that which is sweet,
Sips all the flowers he chances to meet.
The humming-bee buzzing from place to place
Is pursued by this bird and is fond of this race.

The raven was there with his dismal croak;
The red-wing, arrayed in its beautiful cloak
Flew to a branch of the highest tree,

Poured forth sweet songs of melody.
The dove by the side of the paradise bird—
Its cooing to his harsh notes is ever preferred;
But his plumage with magnificence fraught,
As a bird of beauty he's very much sought;
The emerald, ruby and the sapphire doth vie
With topaz to see which is the prettiest dye.

The "Man of War" sails into ocean of space,
Writes his name on the clouds in beauty and grace.
He meets the proud eagle in all kinds of weather,
Soaring so grandly in the star-spangled ether.
In the beak of the eagle is liberty's scroll;
Eventually "'twill wave from pole unto pole."
The flamingo has considerable renown,
With the gayest of pinions to the clouds he hath flown;
He advances with his forces in line;
This wedge-shaped squadron is, indeed, very fine
As they march through the heavens with the back-ground
    of blue,
Presenting a contrast so brilliant to view;
With their rosy-red plumage, these streaks of the morn
Are the banners unfurled in defiance of scorn.
Demoiselle lent his graces and charms
Though some of his tribes are a terror to farms.

The condor is a bird, we will call him the king,
By way of the height that he flies on the wing.
He can give the slightest kind of a snort,
While the ostrich roars like a lion at sport.

The delegates from all tribes and of broods
Came by chance to this part of the woods;
When the great orb of day began to decline,
The birds sought their homes in an orderly line.

The owls in the forest began their "too-woo";
A bird sang a sweet vesper "cuckoo";
"My song is the loudest" said the quaint whip-poor-will:
A parrot more drowsy, bade him "keep still."

The fire-flies came forth ready for dancing—
By their mode of retreat and advancing.
A light could be seen through the darkening glade;
Brighter it grew, as the distance it made
Toward the group, who were viewing this move
In the light of the "Signal of Love."
The "Lantern Fly" has a glorious creed,
Carries its light through forest and mead
To scatter the darkness of sin and wrong,
Says, " Life is sweet as a merry song."
Nature sank to a blissful repose;
Her volume was clasped at the close
Of this day, for now it was still,
Save the occasional song of the whip-poor-will.

CHAPTER X.

The Dream Concluded.

The goddess of morn, arose from 'midst the Sea,
With her "golden chariot" in all her majesty;
Her dewy fingers sparkled brightly in the sun;
Light is divine, for in its rays is Beauty won.

The triad now came forth to view Eden's glory,
Of the rising Sun; to hear Eve's dreamland story.
Said Eve: "I beheld a monarch with a haughty mien;
He was sitting by his wife, her title was a queen.
Isis and Osiris, together with their son,
Formed a " holy trinity," making three in one!

Vishnu was classed with this godly race;
Symbols of his power—sword, lotus and the mace;
The consort of this god, this great and mighty king
Was Lakshmi, empress of whatever wealth can bring.
A lady, I admired, was goddess of the moon.
And all I wished to know, they said, they'd tell me soon;
So, while I was gazing, with wonder and with pride,

At this royal empress, who seemed a regal bride—
'Twas great Diana in which so many towns
Would worship at her shrine in sacrificial gowns;
The crescent of the moon adorned her lovely head,
Flowing robes extended to the ground she tread;
A temple at Ephesus, one of the seven wonders of the
    world,
Was like a magic picture, when they this scroll unfurled.
The girls and women were objects of her care,
The wounded and the sick in their sorrows had a share.

Thousands were before Minerva invoking mental gold—
Scholars, poets, men of fame, all these of royal mold;
Her power will be auspicious in the fullness of her reign,
Her devotees exalted to a higher, nobler plane.
" The better the Deity in wisdom and in love,
The nobler the laity," said one whose name is Jove.
" I saw," said Eve, " those that worship at her shrine,
Arise to be a beacon light, in after ages shine;
This illumination will ne'er expire;
'Twill burn forever, like a torch of living fire.
The coming ages will rekindle this flame
At the altar of this goddess, in the Parthenon of Fame.
Greece, in future ages, of well-earned fame, be proud.
Just then a god's acclaim rang out long and loud :
'Twas Jupiter, that gave this token of respect
To this royal lady, in godly dialect.
' Tis the brightest standard upon our princely walls,
For 'twill be transcendent wherever duty calls.
Said he, " Time will fade and rust,
The escutcheons of the gods will crumble into dust,
Save this, which will be to all mankind
The Central Sun of all the earth—the Sun-god of the
    mind."

The songsters of the wood sang a sweet accord ;
As Eve related all she saw, they warbled at each word
That was spoken, by those reverential lips ;
Eagerly they listened, as the bee his flower sips ;

Nature fluttered in the wildness of her dreams,
Secretly rejoiced at some hidden, unknown schemes.

God said: " My children, I must leave
You, and soon you will receive
Your guest ; must go to my far-off home ;
Occasionally from its precincts will to Eden roam.
So, good-bye ; may the light of future days
Rest upon your heads with my eternal praise !"

CHAPTER XI.

Bird in the Cage.

Eve, while engaged in deepest reflection,
Gave the "Garden of Eden" the closest inspection.
The Edenly birds were all one could wish—
Often declared, " How delicious the fish ! "
The flowers, oft-times, had given her pleasure;
The perfume to her senses a treasure.
The birds knew their mistress at will;
When she was seen their pleasure would trill
In the most happy and sweetest of songs,
That echoed all o'er as a rebuke to all wrongs;
But the enclosure was a fixed, narrow creed;
She saw its expanse was a limit indeed.
Her thoughts would arise in bitter disdain,
Then in a sweet voice sang a plaintive refrain:
"The beautiful flowers—their scent on the air
So humid and stifling!" she cried in despair.
"This Garden is fine and lovely, I know ;
Why this enclosure to limit us so ?
Outside of this pen is the magnificent world."
Indignation was seen on her lip as it curled.
So she concluded on that very day
She would be resigned and thought she would pray:
" My dear Father, please give me some light,
That I may walk in the path of the right ;

Please, give me knowledge, that I may be wise;
I wish to ne'er more my being despise!"
She was more calm on freeing her mind;
Her best impulses told her, a spirit refined
Was with her, like a beautiful mist—
A holy baptism, which she did not resist.
The scene all around changed to a haze;
Streaks appeared with a bright, rosy blaze.
'Twas mysterious, how these luminous shades
Formed into stars of various grades.
"Elysian," was her frank, merry thought,
As, on Nature's canvas, these visions were wrought.
Again as she looked on this painting of air,
Saw a tent and two boys with faces most fair.
"How evanescent! but I would like to know
Who makes these pictures, and whither they go."

CHAPTER XII.

Nature Rejoices.

The next morning there appeared a change of affairs:
Aurora gleamed forth from her ethereal stairs
A crown of splendor o'er the Atlas of earth
A glorious nimbus in excess of the dearth
That's under the dark segment near the north pole
Glowed in radiance o'er the rest of the scroll
Of the heavens.   It was a storm of fine things;
Came like a shower electricity brings.
Could its meaning be Dame Nature's throes,
A mighty endeavor to expel all the woes
That hung o'er the earth, like a funeral pall,
In darkness of mind, might submerge one and all?
The terrified twain were filled with much wonder;
Various sounds, of electrical thunder,
Occurred in the skies of the heavenly dome
Near where their dear Father had built his new home!

They were astonished as all Nature attired
In robes of beauty, which they greatly admired;
Electrical sparks were glinting and gleaming
In profusion, in great splendor were teeming;
Sparks united by some hidden attraction,
Then dispersing by a law of detraction.
Sometimes they would cluster like radiant balls
Which hung from points as pendants in halls;
Again, by the law of attraction, allure;
Electrical columns unite to procure
A temple of *light*, which Dame Nature commands
Each one to observe that her lily-white hands
Ne'er bid us go onward with false, hollow creeds,
But, e'er keep to her charm—the incense of deeds.
Also, these columns, or fiery whirlpools,
Gleam over the land like the light from our schools.
Their attention was drawn down to the river;
The waters were seen to be in a quiver;
Its surface, indeed, by a strange law was stirred
By some great emotion, they really inferred.
Gymnotus, torpedo lent their assistance;
They were inclined to use no resistance.

Eve then glances in a certain direction,
Exclaims in tone of the rising inflection:
"Surely, something is coming. Look, in the East!
Cannot you tell me whether 'tis angel or beast?"

CHAPTER XIII.

A Stranger.

The Devil had traveled for many a day—
Came fast as he could; "for there's something to pay,"
He said to himself, as he journeyed along
The route to Eden, for he did not prolong
His stay by the wayside, and often times said,

"'Do good' is my motto, for evil I dread !"
Way off in another part of the wood
A lyre-bird exclaims in sweet accents, "Do good."
"Do good," said a voice his far-away mate ;
"Do good," chirps the mocking-bird as though he were
    Fate.
"This journey I'll take, for I see through a glass
Not darkly, but well, the hidden morass,
Or miasm, that would breed in that spot
That God has given as Adam's small lot.
Just think ! In a few generations
Would that Garden supply all their rations ?
Am so afraid they will eat of the fruit
Of the "Tree of Life," for it never would suit
The people enclosed in that narrow pen.
No wonder I've come on this trip, through the glen,
O'er the hill-top, mountain, desert and plain ;
'Tis my mission to save all this pain.
Think of the mind to remain a mere blank !
I know there will be foes that never will thank
Me for breaking these numberless chains ;
Helots or slaves they'd prefer to these gains.
Is it a curse to dig in the soil
When in the Garden ? a disgrace there to toil ?
Surely, Adam works by the sweat of his brow ;
'Tis an honor, indeed, to follow the plow ;
To delve in the earth are the sources of wealth ;
Ah ! Hygeia is there, the goddess of health.
I know I'll be trampled in dust ;
Priests look upon me with shame and distrust.
For thousands of years they will ever regard
Me with displeasure—this, my reward !
If I'm covered with false accusations,
'Twill certainly be from wrong calculations.
I'll be rewarded, though late in the day;
Chains I ne'er forged for mental decay.
The wealth of the body and the wealth of the mind

Is the *deed* I leave to all mankind.
But this scheme I must circumvent,
For this I came ; this my intent—
Am doomed for ages to crawl ;
For the sake of mankind, I bide by my fall.
"Fall!" he exclaimed, with a thought of disdain :
"Is it to fall to alleviate pain ?
I've a mortgage on this Garden, or farm,
Which I foreclose without bringing them harm.
Death !   What is it ?   Should mortals recoil
To be set free from earthly turmoil ?
Cut the chains, let the captive be free,
Unloose the fetters, let the prisoner flee
To planes of wisdom o'er Parnassus' height,
Onward and upward in the beautiful light
Of progress and power in the realm of worth,
Where duties claim mortals which call them forth
To do—to act as beings should
In promoting affairs of brotherhood."

Just then he came to a " show of a fence" ;
Surely, God had put no extra expense
Upon its construction, for the brushes and logs
Were crude, but they kept out the hogs
And cattle ; but the Devil now saw
Two forms receding as money at law !

CHAPTER XIV.

The Logician.

Adam and Eve would naturally flee
Under the shade of the largest tree,
When they were nonplussed with this surprise,
Though pursued by Good in ugly disguise.
Whatever it was, gave a dextrous bound ;
Jumped o'er the fence on Edenly ground.

His manner of walking, indeed—it was odd;
Perhaps he was sent an angel from God !
Soon he arrived at the very spot
Where God told Adam not
To partake of the apples, or he'd die;
This, the warning he gave should he seek to defy
His commands, and he told him that day
If he ate of the fruit he'd return to the clay,
Or the earth, in which was his source;
This was his *law;* must 'bide by this course!
The serpent or Devil looked at fair Eve;
Thought, "How much I would grieve
If she and Adam had ever partaken
Of the fruit of Life; should have been quite forsaken !"
As he gazed, with much pride, on this beautiful twain,
The light from his eyes gleamed a fierceness again;
Whenever he thought of the schemes near at hand,
To keep them apart from life's silver wand
Which would give wisdom, love, and truth,
And, a knowledge of science ; this, forsooth,
Will stop the scheme in its infancy—right here in the bud;
So, a little impetulant, came down with a thud.

Said he to fair Eve: "If you will only partake
Of the fine golden apples, please, do for your sake.
To be wise as the gods would be of great use
To all earth's children; then dare to refuse
An order to e'er keep you a slave—
Your mind dark as midnight pent in a cave.
Better let light, with its bright, glowing rays,
Come to thy soul, the rest of thy days,
Than to live as you have with no hope to arise
Above the dear pets you know how to prize.
You know not how slender is the fine, silken thread
Hangs on this event, o'er thy beautiful head.
Accept, and a glory awaits you all o'er
The range of eternity, indeed, ever more

Your soul in its fullness outlive
All curses, that God, in his wrath, ever give !
Now, I'll tell you, he said Adam would die
That day he should eat of this fruit.   I deny
This statement, though, you may judge,
I'm holding for him, a singular grudge.
Not so in the least.   I'll tell you the truth:
You'll live far beyond this day of your youth.
You will see many important events
Take place in a land outside of this fence.
Your name traduced as the author of sin,
You'll be maligned, as really kin
To the Devil, or serpent, in all that is bad
In mischief and evil—please be not sad,
If I give both sides of this wonderful case.
This you should know ere you rise from disgrace !
Thousands of years will certainly roll
On the wheel of Time ere this stain on your soul
Will be erased by Reason's keen lens,
Which is your Saviour from Ignorance' pens.
'Tis as I tell you—your glorious name,
Together with others, will be covered with shame.
Priests will look e'er askance—
Hardly will deign on woman a glance !
They'll teach all the men to shamelessly rule
Women, as though they were babes in a school !
This taint will clog the wheels of Time,
And the far-distant ages will lift this great crime,
As a cloud is rifted by the light of the sun;
Then its waves of delight will flow o'er each one.
When that time comes, women shall be
In their only true sphere of equality.
Man, by force of his manual strength,
Usurps her rights, but her powers at length
Shall win, when the tension is strained,
Too far, for the thread to e'er be regained.
No man is blamed, for Custom is king;

No man is accused of fashioning
The design of life, save priestly rule,
That teaches men in its bigoted school
Their views of life, and the lesson they'll learn
Shall think it right; in time, they will spurn
These precepts they thought were right;
Will give up the shadow for beautiful light.
This is as true as true can be,
That man cannot rise in eternity,
Till he by kindness deigns to redress
The wrong he has done by his selfishness.
When a selfish love, combined with pride
Stands at the altar, by the loving bride,
The bridal veil, of this helpless one,
Turns as black as the cloistered nun,
When he stoops as low as a cruel knave,
Or master, whipping a loyal slave.
I see in the ages that have come and gone,
Man giving woman her right to the throne.
Then he'll sit by the side of his queen,
With no injustice to intervene—
Man and woman side by side,
Onward forever o'er the ocean's tide
Of success, in the kingdom of science,
Where no more rule, or priestly defiance
Will block the route of the lovely pair,
For the golden steps are everywhere."

CHAPTER XV.

The Key.

The largest tree under which they stood,
Was the identical tree that was reckoned good.
The apples were ruddy, large and sweet,
Really adapted for them to eat.
This magnificent tree Eve did admire,

For, to be wise was her greatest desire.
With reverence, she tasted the apple so red,
And gave one to Adam, but he ate it with dread.
Nevertheless, they ate and relished the food,
Readily affirmed the fruit was good.

Suddenly, schools were seen, from the palace down
To the hut, thought Eve; 'tis a sacred town.
Public schools are the solid foundations,
The massive bulwark of all of the nations ;
They are firmly built on a rock,
Securely braced 'gainst priestly shock;
The foundations were precious stones,
Each layer ablaze, or different zones
With glittering, radiant gems
Fitted to adorn youth's diadems.
The costly gems so rich and rare
She saw in this city everywhere;
The walls composed of beautiful pearl,
Sardonyx, emerald and lovely beryl,
Topaz, amethyst and the sapphire
Blending with hues of the striped jasper.
All were luminous in this City of Gold;
These were the schools of the gods she was told—
Gods of Light, Wisdom and Truth—
True guides for the mind of the youth.
The beauteous forms of splendor and grace
Left its impress on her intelligent face.
The Devil watched the process of Good,
Its power so great o'er womanhood:
Said he, "'Twould, indeed, be a curse
On God, angel or man to make woman worse
By his machinations in any one form
That would blast her prospects in life's bitter storm."

While the Devil was deep in grave cogitations
About evil and good in the Congress of Nations,
Adam and Eve went a little apart;

Something in their minds, like a conscience, would smart.
They talked secretly o'er the events of the day;
Were very uneasy, hardly knew what to say;
Like culprits, a law had transgressed;
To hide was their impulse, and wished they were dressed.
What would God say if he should know
About eating apples! where could they go
To escape from his anger? Said Eve, "We will make
Us some clothes; perhaps it will break
The force of the fall, of his bitterest scorn,
For, in my heart, is lurking a thorn!"
They, in appearance, were quiet and grim;
Adam secured leaves from the limb
Of a tree called the fig, for both—
Their first experience in the matter of cloth.
They managed well as they possibly could,
In sewing their garments, with pieces of wood;
All was ready, their toilet complete;
For soon they'd have their Father to meet.

CHAPTER XVI.

God's Sermon in Eden.

"'Tis fine, this grove of sycamore trees;
How bracing this westerly breeze!"
Said God, as in the "cool of the day"
He'd arrived in Eden, having much to say
To his children: "They've obeyed every law—
My commandments perfect, without any flaw!
The true way is to tighten the chains;
Never give them, freely, the reins;
So they remain in their bamboo cage.
What if they do fret and fume in a rage;
Quench all the light in Wisdom's lamp!
My sermon, to-day, is always to cramp
The mind. Let the bells gaily toll

The requiem o'er the death of the soul!
Credulity should be encouraged in man;
This great trait should lead in the van,
So mankind can be led by a string—
Not much work for the priestly king!
Eve talks strangely. I cannot see why
She wishes to travel, and sometime to die!
My fears are she will certainly eat
Those apples; and my scheme will defeat.
She'd like to know as much as the gods.
My advice is, be content, where she trods
On Eden's fair soil where my children will be
Happy as birds, through eternity!
I'll tell her to be ever content
With this Garden of Eden, in any event!"

Rousing himself from his deep meditations,
What an example he'd be to the coming nations!
Bethought where Adam and Eve could be
And anxiously walked from tree to tree;
Passed by the poplar with leaves of unrest;
Broke from the almond a blooming crest;
Thought, "This symbol will ever be
My delicate wand of authority."
Then, somewhat anxious, began to halloo:
"Adam and Eve, where are you?
Tell me, Adam, where art thou,
That you should hide from my presence now?"
Adam replied: "Here am I!"
But trembled in fear of his majesty.
He stammeringly said: "I was afraid of you,"
Forgetting his dress, "and am naked, too!"
"Who told thee thou wast undressed?
Who said this to give you unrest?"
Adam's most plaintive and humble reply,
"The woman thou gavest me," he said, with a sigh,
"Gave me the apples and I, really, did ea t ,

Gravely thought they were delicious and sweet."
God said to Eve, in an angry tone,
"Why did you not leave those apples alone?"
The woman's reply was given in haste,
"The Devil beguiled me, and his logic embraced,
I ate the apples, for my bright, gilded cage
Held a bird of unrest that would often engage
In songs full of sorrow; to be happy and free,
Could only be gained by liberty!"

Just then, the Devil came to view how they stood
In this high melodrama, in this part of the wood.
God saw him, and how he did curse!
Said he: "I am really averse
To all your intentions to baffle my schemes.
I curse you above the cattle that teems
O'er the earthland where they have their abode."
Such was his language, while stamping the road
With his foot, showing the fashion
Of gods when in a terrible passion.
"I curse thee!" said God, while grinding his teeth;
"Thou shalt crawl as the worm on the ground underneath
The feet of man, the dust for thy food;
Thy dowry, henceforth, for the knowledge of good
And evil thou gavest to Adam and Eve,
You'll be divided by enmity, and I bid you leave
This Garden of Eden, soon as you can,
For opposing my wonderful plan!"

"This will not be the last instance curses be given
As mandates from God from the Vatican heaven,"
Thought the Devil, or serpent, just then,
As onward he crawled through woodland and glen.
"Enmity—that exactly expresses
The love that mankind possesses
When their pattern is ' war to the knife,'
Filling the world with sorrow and strife;
Curses, maledictions, 'tis radical hate

That will follow mankind in priestly estate.
Curses I see all along in the years,
Covering the earth with a shadow of fears.
Man armed, cap-a-pie, with this watchword and cry,
'Believe as I do, or you'll be cursed when you die;
Believe as I do, or this bright, burnished steel,
In the name of the Lord, its sharpness shall feel;
Believe as I do, or you'll be burned at the stake,
For not comprehending the presage I make.'
I see millions of people in the name of the Lord
Immolated by the gleam of the sword;
I see battles, carnage and plunder,
As though Thor, the god of thunder,
Had full sway by this terrible crash;
'Tis horror to hear the strokes of the lash.
As I view this dark scene my heart sorely grieves
For humanity, but my conscience leaves
Me blameless.   I know I did well
To open the gate of this theological hell,
And let them out to roam as they will
O'er the plains of the earth, o'er mountain and rill,
To do as they please, in the highway of Mind,
Where treasures immortal they ever will find.
Sometime, I'll have a glorious shrine—
No shadow of curses in this temple divine.
Devil, serpent, whatever it is,
I bide by the name, would not give it for his!
Shall take with me the dearest farewell
Of the scenes around, for that image will dwell
(That beautiful face, so glowing and wise)
In my heart for aye.   This, my prize.
So, Garden of Eden, and Adam, good bye;
I bless you, fair Eve, till the day you shall die;
To God, I would say, no falsehood will claim
Co-partners with the Devil's to blacken your name!
Still, I would say 'good bye' to you, too—
It can't be you know the mischief you do!

Perhaps you are young, and in future know better
Not to forge any chain, handcuff or fetter.
Perhaps you had better be wise,
Something may come to open your eyes !"

While God was so angry—tore each pretty bloom
Of the almond to pieces, while pronouncing the doom
Of the Devil. Eve must expect sorrow the rest of her days.
"Now ceases forever my Fatherly praise;
Your husband will evermore rule
O'er you, and you will be regarded a tool
In his hands; brute force his sway.
As well as the mental, all orders obey !

" Adam," said he, (with eyes flashing fire,
To think all needed the force of his ire),
" Sir, for the reason you were deluded to-day
By Eve, I'll denounce you alway.
Accursed be the *ground;* this soil I now hate;
'Tis your diet hereafter in the world's broad estate.
Thistles and thorns, 'twill a crop for you yield,
And the herb thou shalt eat that grows in the field."

Adam and Eve were like two stricken deer
Near their hunter, who had been severe
In running them down and brought them at bay,
Their flesh torn to pieces by the blood-hounds of prey.
God left them, so they relaxed for awhile
Their statuesque manner, and in hillocks to pile
The leaves, he had strewn on the ground—
Did this for pastime, for in nothing they found
Interest, in Eden, after the curses.
How many tyrants this scene rehearses !
"No matter," said Eve, "harsh words from a Father
Are black as midnight, and, I'd much rather
Be free to roam than be around here;
No, I can't endure this shedding a tear
O'er the past and the present." Surely, her Father she
    dreaded.

So off in labyrinthian mazes she threaded
Her way, in a far-distant nook,
Where she and Adam would never more look
On his visage—God ought to know
That curses were quite mal-apropos—
Thought she, "'Tis, indeed, no disgrace
To give this *key* to the whole human race.

CHAPTER XVII.

Fur Suits.

Said Eve unto Adam, "Please, will you tell
Why the beasts in the forest and dell
Are running o'er mountain and brook?
'Tis a wonderful race; now as I look,
I know the cause of this stir:
They're being caught, perhaps, for their fur.
'Tis God, running so fast;
With his lasso has caught some at last !
He kills them by wringing their necks.
A Hercules viewing the wonderful wrecks
Would have thought them simply immense;
God would have killed them at any expense,
For he quickly knew how to tan
The hides of these beasts for his woman and man—
From this material, cut each a suit—
A dress, coat and pants, even a boot,
Or, sandal; 'twas done very soon—
Ere the dial traced the sun-mark of noon !
They were quite anxious to please
Their Father, to wear clothing like these,
Said Eve, " For the bright, golden sheaves
Showed fall near at hand, and the gay, crimson leaves
Were flying at will; some transformed into gold
Were signs that soon 'twould be stormy and cold."
No wonder they both were elated,

Thinking to be reinstated
In his esteem; still watching his face,
Saw by its shadow, the 'd " fallen from grace,"
For, o'er his brow, did the cloud darkly lower.
" Now, is the time to exhibit my power,"
God exclaimed, " he has become *one of us;*"
The birds began singing, " Please hear his mandamus:"
" One of us," they repeated and a laughing ha, ha !
Said the birds Adam named the macaw;
" One of us" yells the pretty blue jay,
" 'Tis a laughable thing, I really must say."
" Many gods for one throne;" said the cruel jackdaw,
" That are equal with him in matters of law !"
God was chagrined at these demonstrations
Of Nature's tumultuous and harsh exclamations.
He finally said as his august word,
That Cherubims stand with the swift, flying sword
And guard for aye the sacred Life-Tree—
What a fine vocation for angels 'twould be !

CHAPTER XVIII.

Excommunication.

Eve heard a rustle among the dry leaves,
A premonition of something that grieves
The spirit; God is coming with a strange, haughty mien;
He is angry, his eyes flashing keen
On Adam and Eve. They wished much to know—
How long he would be their bitterest foe.
He ordered them to " pass out the gate,
Not by the wayside to reluctantly wait."
The shock was so sudden they stood quite aghast.
Again, the command " to go quickly" was passed.
" Go where?" said Adam, feeling afraid.
" Where?" God exclaimed, " To till the soil I have made;

I have a most lofty disdain,
For both of my children, so, I'll tell you again,
Begone from this Eden where once it was peace;
May curses go with you, and find your release
From all that in life would give you much joy;
Hate the ingredients, this be your alloy!"
They understood him to the fullest extent;
The gate being open, out they both went
In sadness slowly, this beautiful pair.
Where to go, they knew not, but must travel, somewhere.

There arose from the ground an electrical blue,
Fountains of light erubescent in hue,
So imposingly grand, this couple stood still
To view operations of this sign of good-will.
They looked on the mountains that surrounded the dale;
They found kind Nature was rending the veil
That encircled the earth—
For illumination was sending its girth
'Round the globe in one luminous chain
With a glory quite new, to ocean and plain.
A mountain near by was, really, on fire—
Its volume of splendor seemed never to tire.
Others, with their radiant gleam
From their craters, gleefully teem
Their joy; now Homer could rise
With his warriors proud to the very skies.
Vesuvius renewed his wealth of delight,
Erebus spread glory o'er his long wintry night.
How grand was the light of the fiery Tolima!
Sicily inspired by the glorious Etna,
Cotopaxi leaped from his house Ecquador,
A light that shone brightly by his own metaphor;
St. Helens glanced forth in a magnificent flame
That gave to the "States" its quota of Fame—
A tribute like this from the sublime Gualatieri,
"'Tis the gate ajar for the intellectual era."

CHAPTER XIX.

Original Sin.

The Devil arrived at an " exceeding high mountain,"
Drank water from a pure, crystal fountain,
Thought "total depravity" was a beautiful twin
To go with its brother " Original Sin."
Total—those dear ones depraved
Whom I assisted, and finally saved
From perdition ! Whose's to blame; this innocent pair ?
Or the one that should give them his Fatherly care ?
'Tis not wrong to disobey a command
When 'tis known that a hideous brand
Is to be worn to your dishonor and shame
And blacken, forever, an untarnished name.
If woman is willing to remain in a cave,
She never knows fully how much she's a slave.
Let her come out with the loftiest intentions
As a delegate to priestly conventions.
Priests point with disdain at " Original Sin,"
And, tell her " Paul bade her not to come in !"
Priests must say something that they may live at their
    ease
And will not care such a monster to please
As woman; only hide the dark curse
When Benevolence gives them a long golden purse !
These beastly twins with their terrible jaws
Will strip from each Capitol all reasonable laws
And favor dear man because he's so *weak*,
Will need protection or taiff on cheek !
Her birthright—Equality—man will spurn;
Home, a bastile, where a coward will learn
Not to show his eye-teeth or give a fierce growl
And conceal his grim features with a hood or a corol
Of deceit; an underground railroad-divorce
Will vanish as mist when he changes his course.
Let not the once happy wife

Think for a moment of taking her life,
Or glad to advance through Death's golden gate,
For cruel refinement is as cruel as hate.

———

CHAPTER XX.

Great Rejoicing.

Attracted by a mysterious sound,
Adam and Eve walked slowly around
Toward the Eastern part of the fence,
Curiosity being so very intense.
Soon they saw the Cherubims;
Thought God's plans were the queerest whims.
"Why not curse it, as Christ will the fig tree?"
A fairy exclaimed, in the greatest jubilee.

Onward they walked under the shadow of trees,
Their brows being kissed by Liberty's breeze;
The sunlight danced through the branches in glee,
And told by its gleam they were happy and free.
They beheld the beasts roaming over the hills,
And while drinking from the clear, sparkling rills,
Happy were they, for the white polar bear
Could travel northward to his ice-covered lair.
The elephants started in the wildest confusion,
For they came to the sagest conclusion
Their home was in a far away clime;
With speed did they travel to get home in time
Ere the weather become unpropitious;
Thought they, "How delicious
This journey;" looked very sagacious;
"This object was surely tenacious."
The tiger leaped toward his home in the jungles
To a land far away from Edenly jumbles,
To his home that is called Hindoostan,
Where in time, he'll be hunted by his cousin, the man !

The giraffe had a long distance to grope
His way to the Cape of Good Hope.

The sloths walked slowly with their low, plaintive cry:
" Shall go home if we die
On the way; in the tropics 'tis warm;
We shall be free from the cold, chilly storm.
To South America, our journey on trees
Will be peculiar; do not walk on our knees,
But cling to the branches, with the head downward.
It is not our nature to move quickly onward.
When the forest is exceedingly dense,
We go from one tree to another and make no pretense
Of descent to the ground, for each generation
Knows what is best for sloth ambulation.
How it will be, I cannot conjecture,
We can travel so far, is the theme of our lecture,
At this important and eminent crisis
In our lives—the foot-ball of devices,
Such as has been in this place
Where exists the beginning of all the sloth race!"

The dingle enroute for his home in Australia,
Hippopotami bound for some estuary
In Africa—they bade Eden farewell,
Wishing a bath in the water a spell!

Springbok, antelope and bounding gazelle,
Rapid their progress o'er mountain and dell;
Thousands of animals diverging each way.
The howling and barking and the deafening bray
Was a chorus with a weird kind of charm;
All were rejoicing, and, no one would harm.
The various reptiles were in this parade,
For, God, in his mercy, had created this grade
Of animals.   The birds grandly soar;
Their fluttering wings in their vulcan-like roar
Told how gladly to bid fair Eden "good night,"
As onward they flew and faded from sight

In the distance.   The sound died away,
Silence reigned, save the monkeys at play,
And the doves with joy were elate
To be with fair Eve outside of the gate.

CHAPTER XXL

Sea of Splendor.

Eos rising from the Sea, the goddess of the Dawn,
By her steeds divine, her chariot was drawn
From her glittering bed, up from the shades of night,
Drawing aside the curtain, casting roseate floods of light
O'er all the pearly dewdrops that reflected her bright
      beams
In countless glories, that her beauty teems
In majesty; "for every tremulous atom
Speaketh Nature's power that 'tis glorious to fathom
The mysteries of life" said the devil; and he thought
How her mantle by the hand of Nature wrought—
How resplendent when hung on memory's walls
Where we can view this picture on which a lustre falls,
To be studied by the artist, and the philosopher to glean
All the products of her wisdom, by this lamp is glory seen.
There is much to think about in this world of ours—
Speaketh of divinity in the strongest mental powers.
How loud the atoms' voice when heard in thunder tone,
When in proportion to the other forces grown.
'Tis wholly in atoms that are concrete in power—
To work out the mandates force e'er keeps in dower.
No matter, their intonations have one harmonious voice;
When properly understood, maketh every one rejoice.
Her mysteries resplendent, her lamps are neat and trim;
Bursting forth with grandeur is the unfolding of her hymn;
Her symphonies melodious in the extreme,
Harmony is her major key in future to redeem
Mankind from the shady planes of woe,

Up to the mountain-tops of Science' lucid glow.
That, in contrast to a hell of endless fire,
'Tis no pleasant route to heaven, upon his Lordship's ire.
Atacama is this faith—a waste—a mental dearth;
Reason, with its lightning gleam will sweep it from the
    earth.
Then, humanity from priestly craft unchained—
True "Elevation of the Host," when this emancipation's
    gained.
To tie themselves to any post, or circumscribe the creed,
Will securely hold them—will check their onward speed;
This would warp the noblest and purest aspirations—
Keep them in the dust for want of perorations
Of the firmament of the soul's expanse
Where the eagle of the mind can soar with quickened
    glance.
I've no fault to find with priests of godly lore,
Who gladly lengthen chains, and ask in faith for more
Light; who will grow each day and hour
In Wisdom, though in sacerdotal power.
They deserve great credit, for their inspirations tell
On plastic minds of laity while in this purest spell.
Unconsciously they widen the highway 'til it's broad,
And leads by flowery Edens to the pearly gates of God.
'Tis the God of Nature that enrobes them highly now;
Her highest attributes adorn the regal brow.
Not toward them will my indignation rise;
They are godly men that I never will despise;
They are crowned with laurel leaves that burst the
    bands of all
That limits progression in this holy, sacred, call.
Kindness should be the reflection in the cloud,
Of deeds of holy men, in which I might be proud.
'Tis Ignorance, this tiger, that's always in the van
Of the army of unkindness unto man.
"The world is, indeed, my country; my religion is: Do
    good,"

Says colossal Reason, in the name of Brotherhood.
Life's a world of splendor, when each sect is kind, humane,
Climbing ever onward to a higher, nobler plane.

CHAPTER XXII.

Behind the Scenes.

Eve was playing with her pets, watching all their pranks;
Every moment of her life was full of grateful thanks
To one who had redeemed them from desert life;
All was gratitude, with such emotions rife;
Still, there was a shadow creeping through the door
Of her mind's happiness—"events cast theirs before."
She could not imagine why Adam was so queer:
His face was cold at times, his glance was quite severe.
Perhaps, he regretted leaving his home or lot;
Was lost in sad reveries of that strange and godly plot.
She could not understand the true, the vital cause,
'Til Adam came before her; after a moment's pause,
Said he to Eve, in tones quite harsh and gruff,
"You've been playing with these pets long enough;
You must sever all such ties—I'll have no nonsense here;
You must 'bide by my command, or 'twill cost you very
    dear !"
Eve astonished, stood like a statue still and cold,
Her eyes transfixed with wonder, when his wish at last
    was told.
"Can this be my Adam that I thought was good and
    great ?
Am I mistaken—am I in my normal state ?"
Soon she left him, to bear her grief alone,
Where he could not hear the anguish of her moan.
"Oh !" she exclaimed, "this is more than I can bear !
Wish I were in my grave, indeed, or anywhere
Than here ! I thought his love divine—
He was so kind to me. Why this sword of thine

So unmerciful in its progress through the heart?
It stingeth like a poisoned arrow-dart."

The scene around her in this sacred solitude
Quickly filled with fairies, in a tearful attitude,
Bowed with sorrow, and 'kerchiefs to their eyes,
Like parian marble statues, denoting Nature's sighs.
On this occasion were dressed in silver gray,
Trimmed with dewdrops tremulous with this spray—
The lovely naiads, the fairies of the strand,
The nymphs, resplendent, ruling forest land,
Made a mournful scene, these fairies at this time,
Giving sympathy in this mute but rythmic rhyme.

"If this is the way God wished man to rule,
For the first time in life, have been a lordly fool!
Rule, I hate the word; indeed, I almost curse
Myself. I dislike that word far worse—
'Tis all that's low and mean.
This, my vow: No more rule shall come between
My Eve and me; it is daggers to my sight,
Each one crimson with bloody drops of fright.
Never shall I forget the frightened glance,
When I flourished aloft the lurid, ugly lance.
A man who talks to woman as he dare not talk to man,
Is cowardly in motive and falls under the ban
Of dishonor, from the realm of Justice' sway,
And torture awaits him, by Conscience's lucid ray.
Peace has fled; am worse than God
When he displayed the blackened, mental rod;
Hardly know how to act—what course to pursue;
Hardest work of my life, for I don't know what to do.
She may not hear me, e'en should I explain;
Misery, indeed, is this thorny path of pain.
She may spurn me, as, indeed, I ought to be—
Just reward for my inconstancy."

A peri had been rapping so gently at the gate,
Of his best impulses, ere it should be too late;

She succeeded in calming the progress of the storm—
Less terrific this cyclone o'er his form.
A gentle zephyr singing a sweet and hallowed hymn
O'er the spirit, mildly, in one grand requiem,
Of "The Death of Anger"—he falters, starts—"Yes,"
    said, "I'll go;
No longer will I endure this deep, and bitter throe."

Eve seemed floating o'er gloomy, stygian streams—
Was deep in the darkness of Plutonian dreams;
She heard a voice, the accents strange to hear,
Expecting only tones, oh, so severe!
Can it be Adam? saying gently, "Fair Eve,
Please, dry your tears, never more to grieve;
I wish to say that I did the meanest act one could
To any mortal, worse than mortal ever should.
Can you forgive me? Please give an answering look,
To tell me, I'm forgiven; never more I'll brook
Such bitter words that are vultures in the heart,
Tearing out the vitals. How I wish to part
With such company! Then do you, really, spurn
The worm that crawls beneath your feet that he may
    learn
His lesson in regret; in sorrow pass his years?
My dear Eve, I bless you through my tears."
'Twas too much for Eve. She raised her lovely head;
Her eyes spoke her forgiveness; his arms quickly sped
Around his Eve; Love and Love entwined,
On the altar of their noble hearts, were evermore en-
    shrined.
Instantly appeared a million men,
On mountain, in woodland, and glen,
With bugles, clarion, and, flute;
Trombone was there, also, the lute;
Clarionet resounded, with tones of the drum—
All were playing the anthem of Home.
'Tis with harmony where peace can abide,

Where Love is welcome side by side
With its mate—where no storm at this shrine
Should darken the altar; then, love is divine.

The music filled the earth in grandest intonations;
The waves of sound sped around in sweetest incantations;
The tones were full of melody, replete with joyful measure,
That kindness should prevail as life's divinest pleasure.

The fairies, gaily dancing in another kind of dress
Of sparkling diamonds, denoting happiness.
This fairy pirouette was, indeed, full of grace,
And joy was reflected in each sweet and happy face.

CHAPTER XXIII.

God Writes a Book.

A seraph flew to God's abode to tell him all the news
About Eve and Adam. God thought, "I've no time to
    lose,   ,
For the opposing force is powerful to instill
His belief upon their minds by his secret, subtle will.
Can it be, with all this power, I have need of fear—
That the Devil will be king of all I hold most dear?
Will this godly throne become empty as the air,
My rights usurped and me driven from my chair ?
I've work to do—must keep vengeance for my word
As coming from a mighty King, the Great I am, the Lord !
I'll be the God of Battles all along the Jewish line;
All over the Christian land shall gleam my sword divine;
Shall have power to act; shall be in no disguise,
For I am King of earth and Emperor of the skies.
I must make a hell of fire to put my creatures in;
Multitudes will be alive with mortal sin.
I'm a jealous God—no Gods in heaven but me;
No Jesus can thrive upon this godly tree !"
His face was fierce with anger as the prospect viewed;

The glistening gems upon his brow were ready for this
    feud:
"When I see mortals, all o'er the Christian land,
Killing each their brother with the lurid, fiery brand,
Then 'twill be my pleasure to see this loving strife
Taking what they cannot give occult, human life!
Priests will answer with favor in the nod,
'Thou may'st kill,' as a commandment from their God!
'Tis to my glory to have worshipers at last."
His eyes were full of tenderness, as o'er the benches cast
A loving glance, that told how deep his hope
To rule—this heavenly, Christian Pope.
Being suddenly inspired, ordered ink, and pen
And paper—wished to write a book for earthly men.
'Twould be a bible, so pure for all to read,
The greatest work in all the world—what every one will
    need.
Schools will be builded to give children "moral tone,"
"Non-Sectarian," said he, with secret groan! .
Happy were his thoughts, that pleased him very much;
The letters sparkled as he wrought by his saintly, godly
    touch.
The book was finished, and knew what prestige it would
    be,
To make him Lord of all, through vast Eternity!
Laying pen aside, he calmly went to sleep;
He needed rest, but in his visions deep,
Thought of his great exhaustion, on Creation's morn;
Rested many days, so he could be borne
To earth, to visit Adam and his Eve—
Reveled in the thought how he'd grant them no reprieve!

CHAPTER XXIV.

The Devil in Spain.

"Have traveled far to view the land of Spain:
Her history is inscribed o'er all her fertile plain;

The mountains, also the rivers and the dell,
The strangest panorama the rocks and trees doth tell,
I see galleons freighted with her gold,
Wealth and splendor in hieroglyphics bold,
Her vessels sailing o'er all the seas.
As I view this grandeur my senses seem to freeze,
For as I see a dragon traveling o'er her soil,
Tramping with his iron heel, in horror I recoil.
The men who have a conscience, and for this moral right
Are branded as foul heretics, and fall by force of might.
Torquemada, this pure and godly saint,
Liked the Inquisition which would ever be a taint
Upon his name.   What was the Inquisition
But a gladatorial arena of Christian superstition ?
Her beasts fought Honestly at the rack,
Chained Science that it leave no shining track !
Education and Refinement will yet wisely see
The dragon has an ugly mien, to slay his royalty.
This trail upon her ground has made her sadly poor,
Begging for a crust, for she shuts the mental door.
When'er the Church and States combined,
The track of this grim monster will check the empire—
        Mind.
This is not all I've seen with prophetic eye:
In the Land of Freedom he is seeking to defy
The public schools and the teachers brand with shame.
'The immorality' they teach is a stigma on their name.
He's wily and believes that any land
Where Freedom reigns, a Republic cannot stand !
Here in this institution, in glorious Spain,
That is built to torture, manhood will profane.
I see the curses coming on the waves of Time,
Crystallized in their house of brick and lime !
Who's to blame for cursing man or beast,
When such object lessons come from God to priest ?
Hovering o'er America is another dragon's paw,
Having selfish motives in the Courts of Law.

These huge monsters, with jealous eyes,
Think the United States a place to gain a prize !
Put God in the Constitution, and Jesus on the throne,
A ruler of the Nation, and the Holy Ghost alone,
Somewhere ! then they'll have 'peace;'
In this Christian land will knowledge quickly cease;
Vile heretics will give no more impetus to science—
All they will need is, on God to have reliance.
Give the dragons equality in the land,
A battle would prevail in a conflict really grand !
If America will be brave—not be ruled by God or Ghost—
She will conquer all such monsters that invade her lovely
    coast.

Written on the churches, is this quaintest story—
How Piety discovered the land of Purgatory.
In fourteen hundred thirty, at the Council of Florence,
'Twas first found, without the least abhorrence,
By Pope and priests, who wished to be extremely good—
Found *eight* little hells for their loving brotherhood !
Money, from the *living*, would be the *golden key*
To pass dear souls from keenest misery
To Paradise. No wonder the hand of greed
Writes, ' the holy bible the laity must not read.'

' Sell all thou hast, and give unto the poor,'
Is not written upon any creedal door.
This advice is no way to redeem
Mankind, for 'tis an extreme
Which has a priestly glow. Remember gold, as an ex-
    change,
Gilds the landscape with a broader range
Of vision; 'tis as the bee, sipping life's honey
From the flowers of delight—is consecrated money.
' Gold is the root of all evil,' says the giant Fraud,
While demanding fees for the glory of its God !

Now, I behold a lovely queen,
Isabella is her name, and this the scene:

'Tis strange, but true, that men of bible lore,
Ridiculed Columbus and drove him from their door
For teaching this heresy—'that the earth is round;'
Incredulity is learnedly profound
In wisdom; Ignorance scoffs, but the lady of this land
Gave her royal jewels that he might command
Vessels to sail o'er seas, and found a country great and
    vast,
Where Freedom plants her banner in solid rock at last.
The influence of a woman, in this case,
Did much for the disenthrallment of her race.
Her jeweled key helped to break the crust
Of Superstition; time will crumble it to dust;
Science ever conquers in this field,
For *truth* is found upon her shield.
The earth *is round*, and the bible took a rest;
Heresy arose a sphynx, with peculiar zest—
Began anew to investigate
The claims of the bible potentate!
Good bye, Spain! I see better days for you;
Your nobler instincts have beckoned to the Jew
To come within your borders, and freely give their feet
A refuge from some dragon who wants a money treat
By persecution   Many blessings for you, Spain;
Splendor will again be yours, but on a higher plane."

CHAPTER XXV.

New House.

The Storm King warned Adam to invent,
The best way he could, the crudest kind of tent.
The style of architecture was cuniform,
A sure retreat against an earthly storm.

Said Eve, "I had another dream, I'd like to tell:
Was in a land where fairies seemed to dwell;
I saw Jesus who was so very grand;

Could not suppress the wish, so, kissed his hand.
Was told he had his faults—some mistakes were given
In the records of his thoughts on heaven:
The prediction of his appearing in the dome
Of heaven; his pathway from his home
To earth; be in a Sea of Glory ere they should die—
His disciples—'twould prove his divinity !
'Twas a failure; his disciples never saw this glory,
So much like a priestly, legendary story.

Another episode: how a certain law would trample,
In giving this very bad example
Of making water into wine, which is a miracle.
Such modus operandi sounds so empirical.
In early days, traditions were the style;
Priests, of different nations, kept them on file
For use, and general distribution;
This honor to Jesus was by the Alexandrian Institution !

He wore no tiara—no robe of costly lace;
His deeds for humanity were reflected in his face.

The Sabbath law that Moses gave was harsh and cruel:
The culprit would be stoned to death for gathering fuel
On a day so holy; but the great reformer said, ·
'The Sabbath was made for man,' and gladly led
His disciples o'er the temple of his God
Of Nature, doing good upon its sod.

God never rests, and so it will ever be,
All days are holy in the grand eternity.
The Sunday law cannot stop the sun from shining,
Nor tell the cloud to cease its silver lining;·
It can't control the music of the stars,
Nor change the course of these electric cars.
The rain rejoices in its journey to the earth;
The rainbow says, 'no desolating dearth
Shall come to flower, fruit or tree;
The Sunday Law has no power o'er rain or me—
My colors shine as brightly in the seven;

All are holy on the map of heaven.'
Every pagan came before me in this scene,
Exclaimed in horror that Constantine,
A murderer, should dictate the day
For Christians to worship and to pray!

Among the deeds of Jesus, this, the most unusual of all:
Often did he hear piteous moans—a woman's call
For help; these immortal words were written in the sand:
'He that's free from sin, send the missile from your hand
At woman.' Not one was thrown,
For justice was written on each stone.''

Adam thought, how wonderful were her visions in the
        night;
Her inspirations were her guide to what was right.
He could not help, nor cared he to resist
The desire to approach his Eve, and kissed
The being, that was to him great joy;
This was peace, without the least *alloy*.

CHAPTER XXVI.

The Trinity.

When God began to study the import of his book,
His features wore a most puzzled look.
His reflections were, "I love one God the best;
Yet, in my book, are written all the rest:
What did I say—three Gods? What an absurdity!
Yet, one, is three times one, you see!"
Beaded drops of perspiration began to ooze
From his forehead, when about to lose
His senses; 'twas written plainly in his holy book.
His son was there, and his saintly being shook
With fear. "Must not allow him to invade
The kingdom, which only I, have made!
Did not wish to be on equal terms with him;
The son to be the same as I, is very dim.

I have made Isaiah say 'no Savior, God, but me.'
'Tis an enigma, to make this book agree.
Another grave affair—about the Holy Ghost:
This statement worries me the most.
Father, Son, and Holy Ghost—think of such a plan !
This is a brilliant scheme ! no Jew will, or ever can
Believe it.''   For once, he loudly laughed—
'' A new system in the old, I will engraft:
Who will be Christians ? they will like this mystery—
Much to their credit in all their future history !
The more mysterious I make it, for all of them,
'Twill be highly prized, and yet called a ' little gem.'
Though I am a personal God, yet, am everywhere—
Then the Devil will claim a godly share !
This increasing mystery will be the cost
Of millions of people that will be tempest tossed
In doubt; will be engulfed within
A sea of Persecution, for this little sin
Of not believing all that's written in this book,
Impossible to fathom, or, its mysteries brook.''
He arose from his throne, walked briskly through the
    aisle;
His features shone with the most benignant smile;
In merriment wrung his jeweled hands—
The first time, to his page, gave kind commands !
Instantly, became quite pale and wan,
For in his holy book, with the title of St. John,
Says, '''No one hath seen me at any time, nor could they
    live
If they should see me face to face !'   Such a text to give
My people !   What would Adam think, and Eve—
Such an astounding message no thinker will believe !
If a heretic in kindness should teach a little error,
In my book, he'll soon know my followers are Sons of
    Terror.
I shall cease to be afraid or have any serious fears,
What if the earth is deluged with their tears ! ''

CHAPTER XXVII.

The Tropics.

The Devil gave this lecture while in the tropics:
" Here is a fund for various godly topics.
Godly, did I say ?   Not those of written lore
That would enslave the mind forevermore;
Not that kind of gods am I interested in,
But **those** so holy are minus aught of sin.
Such a place among the lovely trees !
Where they love to sing their peans to the breeze.
In her gallery—among the branches green,
Darting here and there are radiant warblers seen.
This choir chants for aye their grandest anthems c ear
'Till the soul in rapture doth revere
Earth's phases in any manner she presents—
Her will, her power, her harmonious intents.
No wonder maelesto is the strain,
So full of grandeur is the rich refrain.
Her chasuble, white as the pinions of the dove—
Fine emblem of her ministry of love.
No soiled priests warping human will,
Circumscribe its force, to Reason say, 'keep still;'
No indulgence sold to build St Peter's Hall;
No sophism to keep members in a brawl.
Nature is a sacred house I reverence, this Tocalli;
In this temple presides the godly Allah.
'Tis a book of science; her pages I adore—
Full of beauty is her written lore.
I kiss thy soil for in our mother's lap
Lies divinity; let me in thy mantle wrap
My form; all is pure and chaste.
Naught to degrade—let me from thy chalice taste
The elixir of life's most consecrated wine;
Thou art, indeed, the Allah or the Vine.
Let me inhale the sweetness of thy breath;
I see glory in the change of death.

All return to thy grateful dust;
The soul climbs in heavenly trust
To a more spiritual state,
Where man is destined to ever imigrate.
No inertia in this grand machine,
Ever in motion, for her destiny is seen
In rock, flower, man; in all her moods,
A kaleidoscope, reflecting, all her goods.
When I look around, mystery is rife—
This one problem: The source of life.
Source, indeed, where can rest the cause—
Where lies the secret of thy laws?
Nature is a volume; let me in rapture read
The source of life. Where is the golden lead?
Science without the least declension
Has traced the cell to the rocks laurentian!
Gazing back to this royal line,
Beauty can be seen in life divine.
With microscopic eye the wondrous cell,
This grandest mystery doth tell.
The 'Tree of Life' glistens with this power—
That the sources of the bird and flower
Are not the same, each living in a temple of its own,
Out of which, it can ne'er be thrown.
How fine is this golden chain,
That reaches onward in the vein
Of truth, up the steps of Time,
Up the pyramid of facts sublime."

CHAPTER XXVIII.

Nemesis.

The sun arose, but how faint the glow,
Climbing as in a firmament of snow—
So pale his light, reflected in the cloud,
Soon to be lost in this aerial shroud.

Nature, in sympathy with this morn,
Donned the robes which were so forlorn.
Take a glance within a certain tent—
Now we know the object of this lent:
In this home a child is born;
This, the reason, Nature is forlorn.
Adam and Eve were bending o'er their boy;
Her pride—his hope— all happiness and joy.
'Tis to them, the sweetest little child !
In their ecstacy, were very nearly wild.
They knew not the symbol of the cross—
A picture, near him, denoting loss
Of some great principle underlying life—
The son of this noble father and his lovely wife.
The words he said, " 'twould cost you very dear;"
Their meaning crystallized right here.
She in her agony "wishing she was dead;"
Adam's anger placed a sword above his head.
Words seem small affairs, but they cost so much,
When poniards in the angry clutch.

Nemesis wrote upon the wall,
This draft of life or protocol:
" The people living in each age,
Think life has reached a wondrous stage
Of civilization; 'twill take long years,
To wipe from earth, some bitter tears.
Tradition like a god of Hate
Told man to rule his loving mate.
If this command had been reversed,
Crime would not be oft rehearsed;
Woman's sway would have more force
In guiding youth in life's true course.
With morals pure as pure can be.
Unmixed by base unchastity—
Rum, tobacco,   Then in the line
Of health, and principles, refine

The spirit; from unwise ways be free—
A blessing to posterity.
Avoid which gives another pain,
A dowry better than the gain
Of wealth, for 'what you sow
Shalt thou reap'—sunlight's glow
Of joy or misery.   Man should not keep
The rights of woman.   He will reap
The tares; for, when Wrong
Sits on the throne, he will prolong
The agitation on Life's sea
As long as exists white slavery!"
"If I'm your slave, my face I'll paint,
As black as midnight's darkest taint!"
The right of kings was held divine;
The negro slave was by this line
Of Justice kept in chains.   Woman, too,
Is held a captive from this view.
Mankind will, sometimes, break the crust
That holds Divinity in the dust
Of Superstition; its right of way
Will be marked by Wisdom's sway;
The clanking chains no more be heard;
Disgrace will claim the unkind word
That's spoken—the angry glance;
Insults are a poisoned lance,
That show ill breeding of the mind—
Course, unfeeling, unrefined.

CHAPTER XXIX.

Pagans.

God concluded to call on his neighbors.
"A cessation from my arduous labors,"
Thought he ; so over the hill,
Wended his way, by power of will.

Soon, he was in their hall of state,
Greeted by gods that were grand and great.
His attention, inadvertantly drawn
To a picture; but the eye of a fawn,
Changed to a tiger's glance,
Asked, "Did that come here by chance?"
"'Tis Prometheus," was Jove's reply—
"Is a God that foes will crucify
Long ere your son be slain,
In the same manner of godly pain!"
The gods enjoying this lordly treat,
Heard him in anger slowly repeat:

"Lo, streaming from the fatal tree
His all-atoning blood!
Is this the Infinite? 'Tis he,
Prometheus, and a God!
Well might the sun in darkness hide
And veil his glories in,
When God, the great Prometheus, died
For man, the creature's sin."

He looked in another part of the room;
If 'twere possible, a deeper gloom
O'ershadowed his royal face;
Toward it started, at a lively pace,
To get a nearer view to see
What manner of painting this could be.
"A woman's picture on your wall!
Have you not read about my Paul?
She has no rights you should respect;
We are the ones that are elect!"
Diana seemed ready to speak—
Full of pity, when he should wreak
Vengeance on those who ever would
Work so well for his brotherhood—
How they would labor in life's turmoil,
These humble, pious pillars of toil.

More, and more angry, God became—
Thought the pagans were very tame.
" This, to her honor," he reluctantly said—
These lines with dignity, read:

" Great Diana! huntress queen!
Goddess bright, august, serene!
In thy countenance divine
Heaven's eternal glories shine.

Thou art holy! Thou alone,
Next to Juno, fill'st the throne!
Thou, for us, on earth was seen;
Thou, of earth and heav'n be queen!
They to thee who worship pay,
From thy precepts never stray;
Chaste they are, and just and pure,
And from fatal sins secure;

Peace of mind 'tis theirs to know,
To thy blessed sway who bow;
Chastest body, purest mind—
Will, to will of God resigned;
Conquest over griefs and cares;
Peace for ever, peace is theirs."

God said, he would bid them adieu,
For he had work he wanted to do!
Minerva thought of Mr. Watt—
Would give word-picture of God as he ought:

" His nostrils breathe out fiery streams—
He's a consuming fire;
His jealous eyes his wrath inflame,
And raise his vengeance high'r!"

CHAPTER XXX.

The Devil in France.

I see cathedrals, costly and rare,
Have been the home of the grizzly bear.

Bartholomew's day is a rebuke to creeds,
When a saint is honored by crimson deeds;
The influence floats o'er every dome—
Pronounces the doom of the Pope of Rome.
Bruno's statue, near the Vatican,
Is an object lesson of his love to man !
Over her borders the refugee
Gladly escaped from fine and fee.
The fagot, dungeon, sword and flame,
All conspire to crush the name
Of freedom—the right to think; but the **hand of**
    Progress
Stays the gait of the prowling tigress.
I see now a noble, old man—
The gifted Voltaire—leading this van
Of a far better army, with no inclination
To take the life of any relation.
If a cloak is made from the hide of the **sheep,**
The wolf is there; if you constantly keep
A dagger—the object, to kill
Any person for the sake of a will,
He judges superior, who freely directs
You to murder as a godly pretext.
The same spirit, has the goddess Kali,
Who wishes her victims to strangle,
        and die
Some way.   Such trophies, her anger appease,
The murderer expects his Paradise fees !
The Thugs are gracious, and very polite;
To strangle and kill, their greatest delight !
"Brothers of Good Will," and "Brothers so Good,"
Are the cloaks they wear in this brotherhood !
The brothers called Christians, are ever elate,
When guiding a throne, or ruling a State.

Here's an episode, on a very small scale—
"'Twould make the visage of savage turn pale:"
Chevalier de la Barra offended a God;

He threw, on a cross, some of his sod !
How was he punished ?   A growl through the screen,
Said to the Law, "By way—guillotine !"
God's anger, no doubt, was greatly appeased;
The dutiful tiger was very well pleased.
An indulgence was granted for the next forty days
To those who'd simply on the crucifix gaze.
In classical Athens, who'd an image profane,
Minerva would look with great disdain,
Upon their City; so, religion, we see,
Is really the same in its strange piety.

No wonder, when the noble Voltaire,
Saw Superstition crawl from its lair
To murder its victims, he thereby provided
A trap for this monster o'er which he presided
With care and attention, by way of the pen,
Which flew on its mission—a lover of men.
This man will be a long time maligned—
His books cursed by priesthood refined.
I see his farm at beautiful Ferney;
Oft to this mecca, in thought, love to journey.
His heart, full of love, bade the fugitive flee
To Switzerland's home, for liberty !

A hundred years' war with its dire oriflamme
Hovered o'er France 'til the peasants' "god dam"
Was a by-word, for the English persisted
To quell proud France, but she nobly resisted,
'Til all her powers were about to expire,
And France lie forever on her funeral pyre.
Joan of Arc came to the rescue of France;
She heard a sweet voice bid her advance,
To save her dear land from deep desolation—
Fast coming to this the French population.
The voice told her, she'd crown him at Rheims
Their king—how like the strangest of dreams !
To be guided by angels, is forever a shame;

And the law of Moses was seen in the flame,
That sent her pure spirit from its temple of clay.
There is, in her honor, a statue, to-day,
Humanity gave, which is better than creeds—
" 'Tis charity's glow in the sunlight of deeds.
The Law of Moses, sweeps down through the ages,
With a terror sublime, as onward it rages;
To the New Testament pays no attention;
Rejoices in the strife of the " bone of contention;"
Never stops to listen to voices so sweet,
The disciples of Jesus were happy to greet.

Liberty, surely, is gaining the day;
She finds her strength in this priestly affray.
Keep watch of this idol; let not l'Infame
Mar this statue, or blacken its name.
O'er this land hovers the hand of a woman,
True daughter of Nature, the child of a yeoman.
'Twill ever remain to give you new life;
To gather new forces, her mission is rife
To develop for woman a higher acclaim,
That will give her honor, glory and fame.

CHAPTER XXXI.

Little Cain.

At first, 'twas a puzzle to give baby a name:
Many were mentioned, proved shallow and tame.
"I know one," said Adam—" *Cain* is the word,
For it is likened to God, or our Lord."
He, in ecstasy, hardly knew what he said;—
O'er Eve there flitted a shadow of dread,
At the thought, "what would become of our boy
If he, like God, should seek to destroy
Our hopes in life's busy mart."
Just then, she noticed their baby, so smart,
Had crept far beyond the door of the tent—

A gay, little captain on this voyage was bent,
Laughingly rowing his own little boat,
" Too soon," thought Eve, " to be thus set afloat."
Adam remarked, " we've reached life's lagoon,
Sailed in the haven to the beautiful tune
Of the dear song of ' Home, Sweet Home,'
Secure from the lashings of ocean's high foam !"

Eve's motives, and each aspiration,
Were first in the crucible, to suffer cremation,
If they stood the test of Reason's bright glare;
She gladly divided the wheat from the tare.
Daily symbols, transparent and fine,
Flowers of light in their essence divine,
Transferred to her spirit a halo of peace.
An arbor so holy gave no surcease
Of joy; she filled up the measure
By giving surprises of beautiful pleasure.

CHAPTER XXXII.

Wine.

" No one must worship the golden calf;
I must not be content with half
My dues," thought God; must be only me,
If I am composed of one times three !
Isaiah says, I form darkness and light;
I create evil which is certainly right;
I bring unto Judah all the evil pronounced—
I'll bring evil upon all flesh I announced.
That's to my satisfaction, entire—
Such wise sayings I greatly admire !
Evil is found in the blood of the vine;
Moses knew I loved the incense of wine,
As it rises to heaven a delicious perfume—
The finest aroma in my beautiful room !
I see in the ages to come,

Temperance fading in the shadow of Rum—
For India, China, and Japan, will fall;
My example, too much for them all !
I roar from my habitation,
To frighten my Israel nation;
To let them know my object is solely
That my heavenly home is very holy !
'Tis a fact—indeed, no William Penn,
Could e'er quell my race of men,
By kindness; was obliged to change
My ten commandments, which is so strange !

Man is king in his Jewish home,
If he wishes his wife to roam
The streets; writes a ' Bill of Divorce;'
This law can enforce
At his pleasure; some will preach
Of easy divorce, but not how I will teach !"
Troy, his page, gave him a note
From Jupiter; this message wrote
To God: 'King of the heavens and earth,
I wish to inform you of a woman of worth,
Whose eloquence wields
A power by her various shields
Of strength—a Minerva in the kingdom of Duty—
A Laksmi in the empire of Beauty
Of spirit—at a temperance meeting
Gave the members this greeting:

Though being Christians, would like to know why
You are deaf to woman's cry
Of distress, and not to redeem
Her from sin; to rise in esteem
Of mankind she's a Colussus most grand,
' A Specter of Brocken' by the wisest command,
E'er engraved on the Cloudland of Time
That shall reap rewards for wisdom sublime.
Though she partakes of life's bitter drug,

Her crimes as black as the villainous Thug,
Have pity, I do humbly beseech,
Ere she's far beyond reach
From sinking in some Stygian lake,
Ere the heart in its angush is ready to break.
Let pity rest in the heart—
A song-bird of love, a music impart;
A word of good cheer to a woman who sins,
For this is the pathway holiness wins.
You cannot arise by crushing another;
A Samaritan for sister, as well as for brother.
How many times has she sought, but in vain
To unclasp from her soul this prison-like chain!
To heaven for mercy in secret hath cried;
Her invocations, grossly denied
By Fate, that custom now gives,
To keep her degraded as long as she lives
In vice and crime, for the fall of the woman
Was the curse given by priestly foeman!

It shows how deep, at this holy convention,
Custom is King, by the following invention:
A Quakeress prayed for her to meet with conversion,
To erase such sins by Christian immersion!
I wish to say, also, to my excellent neighbor,
Who will be first for woman—will labor?
'Tis womanly instincts that will lead by the hand
A sister to the beautiful strand
Of virtue; from the dark waters of sin,
Where kindness will generally win.
I see houses erected in the dear name of Home,
An under-ground railroad where she never will roam,
Save to walk on a far, higher plane,
Never to be seen in dark waters again.
God, King of the earth, and the sky,
I now bid you a respectful good by.

                                   —*Jupiter.*"

CHAPTER XXXIII.

The Devil in the Arctic Regions.

"I love to come on this northern trip,
To view again the 'Devil's Nip;'
With joy I see the frost and snow,
A glorious route where'er I go.
Nature paints with master hand,
Royal pictures that are grand
Upon her canvas pure and white,
Emblematic of the right.

The ice-berg bursting from the shore
Its glacial parent with a roar;
Where it glides the ocean's hue
Reflects the berylline in blue.
It passes onward through the gate,
By crimson cliffs, in royal state.
Every monster when afloat,
Bears freedom's flag upon each boat;
In course of time, when sun-kissed,
Hies homeward in a veil of mist;
When tempest-tossed by cold and storm,
Rests awhile in many a form;
Be congealed as beasts of prey
Or fairy bridge of frozen spray.
Yonder stands the polar bear;
A crouching lion in its lair;
Sparkling flowers on icy trees—
Beauty reigns with quiet ease;
Countless gems adorn her throne,
In this frigid, frosty zone.

A Gothic church, in bold outline—
Arches draped in flowery vine.

A flat-roofed temple, is the style,
Like one reflected in the Nile.
Columns gave each door or gate

Hue cerulean—quite ornate.
Huge ice-floes clash and grind,
Resounding on the Arctic wind
Like a storm at sea,
Terrific in its majesty.
Ice-floes tinged with gold,
Purple seen in every fold
Of icy robe; peaks arise,
Lost in heights of sappharine skies;
One resembles the spire St. Paul's;
One, by immersion, Niagara Falls.
Holy Water, is seen in the air,
Sparkling in light, most everywhere;
It sweeps through the sky in manifold forms,
Reveals its glory in earthly storms;
It falls to the earth in diamond dew,
Reflects its mission in lovely hue;
It dances down the mountain side,
On to the sea in regal tide.
Each fountain exclaims, 'I am divine,
For I give life to flower and vine.'
Neptune, from his home in the sea,
Says, 'water is holy as holy can be.' "

CHAPTER XXXIV.

A Mystery.

What can this mean—Nature ablaze
With glory, in this luminous haze !
Fungi, a phosphorous light,
Are lamps at this time of night.
Nasturtium, marigold, poppy,
Emit flashes of light, to copy
This example, which is not silly,
Exclaims the electrical lily !
Rhyzopoda, like lava on land,

Great numbers are seen on the strand.
Now they're afloat on the sea—
An event transpiring, what can it be?
Annelides white light doth evolve,
A mystery would all like to solve.
Tunicata in the tropical seas,
Made waves of light in the midnight **breeze;**
Glow-worms of every descrpition,
Fire-flies by Nature's conscription,
Lent their magnificent charm —
Should have no fear in these harmless **alarms.**

Meteors, too, of various sizes
Were striving for luminous prizes;
Some, very large, were brilliant as **suns,**
Others bursting, their noise like guns
In war in a brisk cannonade
Were the voices in this cavalcade!
Beautiful, majestic and grand,
They shone o'er the sea and the land;
Some carried in their meteor train
Pellucid light or luminous mane;
One on the ærial march
Of igneous crimson formed an arch,
Iridiscent as a beauteous bow,
Over a tent this electrical glow!
Lumen Boreale or streaming lights
Were seen in their various heights;
Pyramids and flaming spires
Were formed by electrical fires;
Some truncated or reached half way,
Others to Zenith in a flaming ray.
At times, a whirlwind girate,
Then pass to another state
Of blazing lances and pillars o' blood,
Assume these shapes in this fiery flood.

Joy reigned in the tent, for this little **fable**

Would not be complete without brother Abel.
"This is a child," said the dove to its mate,
" Of love, by order of Fate;
Nothing wrong here, for he's a love-child—
No brand of oats running wild.
He will be worthy his name—
He never will live in the shadow of shame."

CHAPTER XXXV.

Troy.

When Troy went to the Pagan forum
He thought it sanctum sanctorum;
The pagans treated him kindly—
Were never in manner supinely
Indifferent about working, but planning
Schemes for good, and mentally scanning
The earth-plain, to ever devise
New plans, and wrong ones revise.
Troy saw this, and liked the plan;
He was fast becoming a noble man.
Their gods were not perfection—
Were war-like some; by close inspection
They were not such godly terrors
As some are shown by priestly errors.
He saw the jealous defiance
The Christians held for pagan science.
The Christians taught the earth was flat;
The pagans knew much better than that,
So taught the earth was round.
Christians concluded with minds profound,
To destroy the priceless pagan books;
God's wrath was appeased by their cheerful looks!

Troy told God they were busy as bees,
In the hive of industry, trying to please
Humanity, by giving astronomical signs

And problems. also in geometrical lines.
Would impress Euclid and many others—
Be a great chain of intellectual brothers.

Women would be greatly inspired
In science; philosophy in wisdom attired
As queens in the realm of mentality—
A galaxy of stars in the dome of reality.

Keep this creedal plank in view—
Wine they teach to e'er eschew.
'Tis poison, to the crimson flood—
A lurking serpent in the blood.
A chart should be in every school,
To see this serpent in the pool
Or blood; colors change from pink to black;
The stomach's lining is the track
Of vipers, when in the "tremen's" wrath,
Hiss along the darkened path.

Teach a child to e'er rely
On manhood's strength and purity;
Let will-power give it self-respect—
No lovely attribute reject;
Live to be a source of light,
A guiding star for all that's right.

CHAPTER XXXVI.

The Devil's Museum.

Calvin said, "the bible contains
All knowledge, and science profanes
The mind." Did Copernicus teach the sun stood still
That the people might plunder and kill?
Did he tell beautiful tales
About Samson, Jonah and whales?
His science taught the earth revolves
On its axis, and numerous resolves

Were made to quiet their fears;
Kept him for thirty-six years
From printing his book;
Gave pagan science a savage look.
Melancthon claimed the bible to teach;
"Joshua's astronomy is all one need preach!"
Cassini, the Dominican father,
Said "the Devil's the author
Of geometry;" the Church did promote
Him; Bishop Fiesole, his vote,
The same; Gallileo, in a dark inquisition,
Found his exalted position!
"I'm the author of the gift of astronomy,
As well as the science, geology.
It conflicts with a godly style
Of creation; who e'er heard aught so vile!
I glory in my Devil theology—
This wonderful science geology.
Medical science, opposed by the church;
They were ready to search
For the Devil. St. Augustine
Taught 'twas too sacred to glean
Knowledge of the science anatomy!
Disease, an anamoly;
'Tis better adjusted
By God—not to be trusted
To man. Pope, Innocent III.,
Forbade surgical work—this Infallible Word!
Pope Honorus, against it as well;
Dominicans banished books that would tell
Such terrible truths; Pope, Boniface VIII.,
Said their greatest physician had the Devil's faith!
These are my professions;
Now give my honored possessions.

This invention is a Fanning Mill;
The church declared 'twas against the will

Of God; let come what may,
The wind should always have full sway.

Lucifer matches, an emblem rare,
For light shall spread most everywhere!

This boat propelled by steam,
Is an invention, I deem
To be useful; the church did oppose
This vile heresy—that terrible woes
Would accrue.   God said the mail
Should go by way of the wind and the sail!

The next invention, I confess,
Is also mine—the printing press!
Here, I see the light of flame—
Prometheus' torch in lasting Fame.

CHURCH INVENTIONS.

On this door you see the Dove;
Within are symbols of God's love
To man; Justice whispers this to me—
' Here lies one source of heresy !'

A *Collar* is the first I'll show
You—an invention; priests know
How on the neck 'tis worn.
Imagine the suffering borne
By the victim; iron points, you see,
Soon hurls them out of misery !
Here's a virgin, doll-like—
Contains many an iron spike;
Clasps Heresy in its *loving* arms
'Til death ensues by priestly forms!
Many holy inventions are in this room,
O'er which Bigotry pronounced the doom
Of the heretic.   Where do all the curses lie ?
Who gives blessings—God or I ?
Will they pour their holy chrism,
On the sainted head of Spiritualism ?''

CHAPTER XXXVII.

Face to Face.

In process of time, Abel and Cain,
Were young men—good boys in the main.
Abel tended the cattle and sheep;
Cain worked in the garden, to reap
What he had sown—the seeds of the wheat.
At even, they heard their father repeat,
The story how God had created
The heaven and earth, 'til they rated
Him a wonderful God.
Why did he not visit their sod
Again? would it not bring
Him, by giving an offering?
This, too, would his anger appease;
This would certainly please
His majesty; so Abel, to prove,
Brought his sheep to see if his love
Would descend; Cain, his fruit,
The best he had—'twould suit
Him. God quickly came;
Why did he not treat them the same?
Abel's gift was greatly respected;
Cain's was in anger rejected!
Why such treatment from his noble relation?
This gave him his first, his only temptation.
Not being well-balanced, he sailed down the stream,
Without a struggle to try and redeem
Himself from the cataract steep,
O'er which, he would suddenly leap
Into the dark waters below.
"Ye reap always as ye doth sow."
Cain and Abel went into the field;
Cain was wroth, and would not yield
To better thoughts than discontent,
So on poor Abel his anger spent.

Abel said kindly, "perhaps the next time,
He'll do differently, or help you to climb
Out of such feelings; please be not sad."
Cain looked like God, he was so fearfully mad!
I'll teach you not to talk to me soft;
A club in his hand, which he held aloft,
Descended, killing poor Abel.
The brand of the murderer's label,
Cain had to wear, to be his, during life,
For not quelling in time, this feeling of strife.

Cain was astonished at the terrible deed!
Quickly God came.   Did he try and lead
Cain in a better, and far nobler way?
Did he tell him such an affray
Was hurtful—'twas better, by far,
To be good, and never to mar
His soul by such unboylike transactions,
Which, in their nature, have no attractions
For just people?   'Twas quite the reverse;
He stood there, and did nothing but curse,
'Til in agony, said Cain, " I declare,
'Tis really more than I'm able to bear!"

Pity the boy, for who's really to blame,
For bringing this sorrow, anguish and shame?
See Abel's body lying cold at the feet
Of God and Cain.   Vengeance is sweet
On an offender—his curses to shriek;
This manner ungodlike, and weak!

All over the mountain and hills,
Were seen the rack, the stake; and the rills
Were gory as the beautiful Seine,
When thousands of Huguenots slain.
The glaring axes of the dread guillotine,
In great profusion, were seen,
To lend their aid in this holy slaughter,
Where blood flows freely as water.

The Duke of Alva is bearing the cross—
Slays without mercy, 'til the Netherlands loss—
Fifty thousand men and women,
For a little difference by way of opinion!

The Waldenses were followed for many long years,
Having no pity for their sorrow and tears !
Beaten with clubs, on the rocks are they killed,
Thinking a foundation to build
Of the Church of God, which will better secure
From his wrath—he, so holy and pure !
At last, these fugitives flee
To dark, dismal caves to see
If these fiends could possibly avoid,
Ere their numbers be wholly destroyed.
See Holiness building those terrible fires !
At the mouths of the caves all life thus expires !
Four hundred infants are dead in one cave,
With their mothers, in this holy grave !

Behold, the great Charlemagne,
Is a Christian, by the number slain
At his command; his career
Is marked with bloodshed, carnage and fear.
Only the duration of thirty short years
Did he murder, 'tis to his glory appears.
He carried the banner—the religion of love—
Believe or be killed, as the command from above !

Again, o'er the hills, are various raids,
To recover a city by holy Crusades.
See the suffering, the murder and loss,
All to reclaim the home of her cross !
'Tis done for the glory of God—
This the way that's narrow, not broad !

Simon Montfort, the "Churches' Avenger,"
Received a commission against every offender
Or heretic; well did he plan,
To ruthlessly murder his brother-man.

England, with her flaming sword,
Carries the gospel—the bible, her Word,
To slaughter the harmless Sepoys;
Such religion, she ever enjoys.
See, all along, how the colonies bleed,
By the holy example of this Moloch of Greed !

Russia holds her cross very high—
In vain the fugitives from her myrmidons fly;
How many are sent to those terrible mines,
In Siberia !   Where is there a shrine that refines ?

Flames arise from the fagot and stake,
Thousands dying in this sulphurous lake.
Millions of people are slain,
Which to the thoughtful, is plain
Love never murders nor kills;
No blood in the beautiful rills
Of her empire; in her school
Is found the light of the Golden Rule.

CHAPTER XXXVIII.

The Devil Visits Mammoth Cave.

"Am now in a wonderful grave;
'Tis Nature's—the great, Mammoth Cave.
'Tis the largest in all the earth plain—
Worth while to come here again and again.
A sarcophagus, where are beauties entombed;
Nature's grotto, where flowers have bloomed
For thousands of ages in ossified form;
Glory effulgent where the wind and the storm
Held no sway; still, Beauty is here—
Her reign we should ever revere.
Go to the tropics—it adorns the fair earth—
A gem-laden belt or flowery girth;
Go to the Northland, we see the pure crystal
Sparkles in light in the baptismal

Font or the vapors—the snow and the rain—
Her dominion extends o'er all the earth plain.
In this part of the cave, the ceiling is high;
Stars glitter as in the dome of the sky;
The columns extend to the floor;
Fluted, are they, and I greatly adore
Their splendor—some grotesque,
Ornamented in style arabesque.

Graceful festoons show in the light
Diapery resplendant and bright.
'Tis an underground city, with long avenues,
Extending each way, with its various views;
So beautiful, I've not described
Tithe of the perfection of its art here inscribed.
Sculpture stands forth in relief,
(Transcendent beyond mortal belief,)
So perfect, so fine in all of its splendor,
'Tis a pleasure to come here and render
Thanks, for here's glory enshrined,
And various forms of beauty combined,
That we may adore wherever we trod
This earth—Nature—our God.

' Fairy grotto,' doth gaily assume
The fantastical in its beautiful room.

' Star Chamber,' with no priesthood severe,
To sign death warrants are ever found here
To tarnish a record or code,
With crimson, in this blissful abode.

' Vulcan's Forge,' by the absence of fire,
Denoting frail gods will expire
Or vanish in darkness and gloom   ·
By the color of crepe in this room.
The 'Chapel' seems a temple divine
Where Jesus would pray at this shrine
In secret, thus illumine his soul
With majesty, power and self-control.

Here's a 'Pulpit' and the Devil's 'Arm-Chair'
At peace, at last, these opponents of air.
'Hercules' Pillars' denoteth strength,
By the superior length
Of these columes; then, 'Valley Humility'—
Have to stop with the greatest timidity,
For fear of striking the head
On the rocks.   'Winding Way,' is something to dread
By tourists; perhaps is a test;
Like Mohammedans, invest
Their peculiar religion,
With this superstition.
To obtain a pass to Paradise shore,
No morals required on this narrow door—
(Two columns standing quite near
Each other;) though the trial's severe—
Try to squeeze through the gate;
The *men*, pass to a heavenly state.
'Flora's Garden' has snowy flowers,
Beautifully wrought, as in fairy bowers;
Roses and lilies in the greatest profusion,
In Nature's parterre, in holy seclusion.

Another room, as it greets my vision,
Exclaim in delight, "this is elysian!"
No monarch or king in the land,
Could such a palace command
At his pleasure; the diamond glow,
Rich in their glory, in this region below.

There are rivers in this wonderful cave,
So placid, not a ripple or wave
To disturb their waters; as I go down the stream
Of the Jordan, my senses teem
With delight, as I view the arch
That contracts on the onward march,
'Til I bow my head in fear of the rocks—
These massive walls of granite blocks.

Now have arrived at Echo River;
Here I'll pause and deliver
Praise to Nature; reverently bow
To all such splendor; secretly vow
To learn and live by this power of love
That is around, beneath, above.
I bless mankind—I utter slowly—
'I bless mankind,' said the echo lowly;
'I bless mankind,' said it again—
Was repeated in a hallowed strain;
Rich the murmur as it died in the distance—
'I bless mankind,' for his earthly existence,
Will be repeated by the echo of love—
A message of light, wherever we rove."

CHAPTER XXXIX.

Abel.

God said unto Abel, "'Tis curses you'll know,
Will fall on mankind, deep as the snow
In winter; 'twill fall very deep
For their sins, and suddenly leap
To their homes in that land
Where sulphur oozes from the hot, burning sand !
Here, in this bible, it often occurs,
As coming from God in ermine of furs.
I am the one who issues these curses;
Will give mankind their horrid reverses.
God turned to a chapter that suited him best—
The twenty-eighth he was in quest,
In Deuteronomy; curses aglow on my pages,
My wisdom to soar on the pinion of ages,
Like vultures to frighten them in
My fold—secure from all sin !"
Troy said to Abel: " By that elocution
Would follow dire persecution."

God said—" I've power to cleanse all stains—
Could, if I would, bind the Devil in chains;
But this is their fees:
Non-believers must reside in Hades!
Abel, by your mother's great fall;
The rest of mankind, no matter how small
The infant, will live in perdition
For your mother's sedition!
No one can come to my heavenly throne,
'Til Jesus travels to earth alone—
Along with me—and not with me;
Not quite clear, this pedigree!''
God, for a moment, gave his book a review,
This contradiction seemed to be true.
He saw the bridge, like the rainbow's span,
Was the spiritual highway 'tween the rainbow and man;
But he lulled his conscience in the usual way,
" My people don't think, but only will pray!''
To Abel, said he, "go from my lordly domain,
Nor dare to visit my dominion again!''
Abel departed, very much grieved,
To be so unjustly received.
" My mother fall," was his cry of disdain;
" My mother fall," his heart full of pain.
" What great sin could my mother do?
She, always so noble and true.
She is my idol—I love her so well;
All of us live in the dark dungeon of hell!
I scorn the assumption—I know there must be,
A home somewhere in good company.''

CHAPTER XL.

The Devil in England.

The "Magna Charta" of King John
Was, in fact, republican.

The despot's throne received the wave
That lashed with force the tyrant's grave.

As I glance o'er this domain,
The dragon's eyes I see with pain;
I see him chase with fiery brand,
Pilgrims to a foreign land.
Henry VIII., a modest king,
Appeased his Lord by offering
Many souls as a sacrifice
On the funeral pyre of his cruel vice.
This protestant king, with loving grace,
Beheaded two wives to give a place
To others; two gave a bill of divorce.
And two died, by the natural course
Of events. This "Faith's Defender"
Has a record full of royal splendor!
The Church of England cannot claim
Its source is free from sinful shame.
No follower of this saintly king,
Should deign to give a cruel fling
Of rocks at woman, who's ope'd the door—
Resolved to be a slave no more.
Divorce exclaims: "That woman's name
Soars above some legal shame.
The Dove that's wedded to a crow
Cannot be spotless as the snow,
When in his power, to bide his will
When 'tis used for wrong or ill."

Cobbett writes, with telling power,
Of Innocence traveling to the tower
Of London, and the stake
Arose, aflame, as from a lake
On fire; their shrieks I hear—
Killed for the God they loved with fear.
The Protestant child was like its mother,
In slaying with care an innocent brother.

Their numbers, writes Cobbett were visibly less
In England, by deeds of holiness.

Another chip from the saintly block,
Landed quite near the Plymouth Rock.
Their laws were blue as blue could be—
Many were hung on the " sacred tree."
Roger Williams, the first to claim
The right to think, and for this shame
Was driven forth, in sleet and snow;
The religion of love told him, " to go !"

No wonder this religion, so lowly and meek,
Could not rest on the crowning peak
Of the Constitution; this God of the Air
Could not rule in a Freeman's chair.
Now I behold another scene—
A throne, a lady and a queen.
I see upon her dazzling crown
The gem that gives her most renown,
When she refused with golden pen
To help enslave four million men
And women.   Light transcends the kohinoor—
Her heart in sympathy with the poor.
This noble queen, with pen of flame,
Inscribed on every heart her name;
In America, gave her prestige as a queen,
Whose influence rises in a sheen
Of splendor, beauty, grace—
A lover of the human race.

CHAPTER XLI.

The Brothers.

Abel was aware of his mother s great grief;
Oft had he sought to give her relief
From sorrow.   Emotions of dread
Would vanish, at times, at what the Devil had said

A great while before, said she, in the gloom
Of her grief: "Wish Abel would come to my room."
He came; a vision was revealed to her sight—
A sweet, sainted face illumined the night
With a halo around him that gave her deep peace;
Shadows vanished, which proved a release
From trouble. "Death," she thought, is life's golden
    gate,
Through which we'll pass to a heavenly state.

Abel went to see his dear father—
Found him quite sad. Said Adam: "I'd rather
Give my life, than have our loved boys
Plunge us in grief, and engulf our joys
In darkness, in some deep abyss—
Entomb our hopes and all our bliss."
He received an impression; glanced to the sky;
Thought a sweet presence to be very nigh
Him. "Must be," thought he, "a home,
Where we shall meet Abel, when e'er we roam
From here. I'll bide my time,
When to our dear boy, in gladness will climb."
Abel was joyful that he had given,
His parents a glimpse of his heaven.

Abel found Cain in the toils of remorse;
Its whip lashed his spirit with terrible force—
In anguish, exclaimed, "why did I take the life of
    another?
Why did I kill my own, gentle brother?

Abel, if you'r living, can't you forgive
Me, and inspire me to live
A better life? Pure emotions, from some angel-soul,
Seems hovering near, to gain full control
O'er my impulses. Shall, in future, redeem
The past: in this hallowed gleam,
I know I'm forgiven,
For light has descended from heaven."

A large institution arose to the view—
A price commodious and new.
Prisoners, used firm ly, as Justice demands;
Kindness, the rule, by the higher commands
Of the soul; by some cause and effect
They've lost the bright star of self-respect.
The cause, may arise in the foun ain or rill,
Where the poison was drank, and the power of will
Was broken.   So ever be kind,
In helping those who are morally blind.
Cain wished to travel; said, "I must go away,
From the home, where that bitter affray
Will not haunt me; where peace can abide,
At some other home, by my own fireside."
The parting to all was a terrible trial—
Must be borne by great self-denial.
Cain started with his cattle and sheep;
His father gave him some fruit to keep
Him from starving; he bade them farewell—
In a strange land, hereafter, would dwell.

A few miles he traveled on Nature's fair sod;
He came to a city, indeed, it was Nod!
"People here!" he exclaimed: "how can that be?
Thought no one existed but our family!"
Look at those houses—I can hardly be ieve,
Such a city was builded; who could deceive
Us?   Here's a large caravan;
Will ask, if they possibly can
Tell me, where are they going?
Where they live, will be well worth the knowing."
When they came near, said—"I'd like to ask,
(If it would not be too much of a task
To answer), where are you going; where do ou live?
And a sheep, for y ur trouble, I gladly will give."
The man replied: "I care for no sheep,
This knowledge you can keep

At your pleasure: I'm bound for a land,
Where the people are many and grand
In laws and physical science,
And would bid defiance
To any nation, that would in learning excel;
In Egypt, is the land I love so well!"
Cain listened; his wonder was great,
To think such a prosperous state
Could be so large.   Onward, he went,
Thinking, 'twas strange, who could invent
Such a story as Eden.   "Well, now have arrived
Near the city; my cattle have thrived;
Now will plant me a garden—
Install myself as yoeman, or warden
O'er my possessions: a wife I will get.
Really, I may see happiness yet!"
In process of time he was duly married;
Poor Cain constantly carried
That one bitter thought, notwithstanding this scar,
His spirit shone forth a bright, shining star!

CHAPTER XLII.

The Devil in America.

As I journey o'er the Sea,
Toward the home of Liberty,
I stand in rapture at the scene
So grand, so holy, and serene
Rests Liberty; on fair Bedloe's isle,
A statue raised in gorgeous style,
Showing Republics love each other,
As mankind should a loyal brother.

The Dragon's voice roars o'er the land—
Exclaims, "Republics cannot stand;
Have faith in Jesus is their cry,
Then at any time are safe to die.

For morals are no passport given,
To live at last in great, high heaven."
Their creed, indulgence gives,
To the believer while he lives
To sin; for *faith* alone
Wafts them to some holy throne.

He that res s s temptation's sway,
Has made his spirit bright as day;
Is honor'd by the poison d dart
Of scandal's cruel. hear.less part
To *kill* the one that dared to be
A god of vast morality !

Jesus saw with great disdain,
The narrow limits they attain,
Who build a fence around a few;
No matter whether Jew
Or Gentile; he was known,
To treat all nations as his own.

Priests have echoed at a'l times
' Heresy is the worst of crimes';
To give their fo''owers moral ease,
Excuse to do quite as they please
With those who think and reason well—
Mind's outgrown the mystic hell.
Withhold, awhile, your fee of gold,
The priest sends you from the fold
By his saintly. martyr frown.
Jesus has no harp, nor crown,
For such to wear.   Jesus loves fine **dress—**
Seems to increase his happiness !

" Republics cannot stand ?
See the towering Switzerland;
She had her grand " Thermopylae,"
Which gave her strength in Liberty.

Hark, I hear an eagle scream;

His flight is like the lightning gleam;
Two crimson beasts are on his trail—
Finds no rest when they assail
Him; so on they fly—
These twin monsters of the sky.
One exclaims, in thunder tone,
"Jesus must be on the throne;"
The other, with terrific yell,
Wants to stop the school-house bell
From ringing. Public schools must shut the door;
Ignorance, be their classic lore.
Again, the first: "I'll rejoice,
When unbelievers have no voice
To take the oath, or ballot give
To men that really should not live!"
Together, sing this merry song—
To work or play is very wrong
On the holy Sabbath day;
Mark this, what Jesus had to say:
" My father works, and so do I,
Good for great humanity!"

The birds sang this hymn of joy,
That God lets them all employ
Their freedom, as they will,
In songs of love, in merry trill
On every Sunday of the year.

The flowers, without aught of fear,
Exclaimed, "all days are holy as can be
To those imbued with purity.
Gentle lambs skipped o'er the hills,
Sweeter sang the mountain rills,
When Jesus gave this fine ukase:
" I'm opposed to those that praise
Infinity; all days are holy, when good deeds,
Rise above the musty creeds."

The Confederacy, thought to please

Its God, so were at ease
When it launched its Ship of State.
Had God written on its slate,
In love's name the guarantee
Of success is Liberty?
Sometime the dragon's voice will cease;
Then will reign that perfect peace,
That is formed when love transcends
To higher planes, with freedom blends.
The eagle is in Washington,
A regal bird to look upon,
When Freedom rings from every bell
Superstition's final knell.

CHAPTER XLIII.

Fate.

God saw crevices all over his room,
Thought the day of his doom
Had come; snakes glide along.
"Must be something wrong,"
He exclaims—Hear the loud rattle,
Like reptiles engaged in a battle!"
Some said, with a powerful hiss,
"Curses will give you much bliss,
No doubt." Horror was deeply depicted
Upon his face, to think he was convicted
By his own creation. "O, what shall I do—
The Dragons are coming in too!"
"We've come home to roost, said each writhing snake,
Like chickens, for we wish not to break
A law that is as certain as Fate·
Curses will return on your own Ship of State.
Increased is the army by fine volunteers
To remind you the Hate you've hissed forth for years!"
This saintly and godly laocoon,

Struggling for life by the power upon
Him, (but his over mastering conceit
Would prevail,) sti'l would repeat
The curses, 'til they were the cause of his doom
Of death, for the *curses* were engraved on this tomb !

*   *   *   *   *   *   *   *   *

Oft had Abel been to see his mother—
To see them all; was proud of Cain, his brother.
It being the course of nature, his mother was to die—
Then would live with him in the highlands of the sky;
They together would roam
O'er the emerald hill-tops, and visit many a home—
See Nature's temples in spiritualistic forms,
Safe from priestly, cyclone storms.
Fountains of splendor in great beauty rise,
Lovely statues, sculptured in the skies,
Children learning wisdom from emblematic fountains,
Tints of pearl surround the spray-like mountains,
The color in the stream group from blue to rose—
From rose to yellow, in which the spirit grows
(Whether earthly, or one lives in heaven)
In knowledge, wisdom to such are given.
Blue denoteth wisdom; all these combined,
Form white—perfect truth—the sun-god of the mind.
When white is tinted with the rose,
The child is pure and loving—spirit grows
In beauty; when this tint is with the blue,
Is wisdom, purity—to every one be true.
White, shaded with the yellow—that child is very pure;
Universal knowledge t will e'er secure
From any source.   Be patient, with the child
That asks so many questions—almost turn you will
When many hues are blended with the white,
With a rainbow edge, 'tis a halo very bright,
Denoting various gifts that form a bow
Of splendor, where'er the child may go.

Falsehood, creates a streak of black:
To soil this aura, leaves a darkened track.
Anger, will impress a blackened shade;
Repentance, will cause it all to fade.
A generous thought, or one stained with sin,
The ambient air, reflects the temper you are in.''

Abel soon would have his mother with him, to see
The beauties of his world; very quickly, would be free
To view the people, that were already there.
Civilization on the earth was almost everywhere !
Baalbeck existed, and her temples grand,
Famed for their splendor on Phenician sand.

Egypt, flourishing in all its pomp and power—
Temples in India Heavenward did tower.

Central America, with her Teocalli—
Many costly fanes contained a godly Allah !

Soon was Abel at his mother's side;
Adam, full of sorrow—how the child cried !
Abel, so happy, could not know this grief.
Patiently waiting 'till she found relief
From pain—said Eve, ''I saw Abel's face;
He appeared so happy, I could plainly trace
Every feature.''   She kissed them; one and all;
Her spirit released, some one seemed to call
Her name.   'Twas Abel; her own loved boy;
Both cried in their excessive joy.
Mother, in the arms of her dear son—
A glorious scene, sacred to each one.
They soon arrived at the cottage door;
In thankfulness, paused to adore
Existence, in this universal plan—
The final redemption of every earthly man,
To rise secure from mortal pain—
To live, for aye, on this seraphic plane.
Within the precincts of this portal,
On the petals of the flowers, was the word immortal.

Birds sang their "Welcome" in the sweet refrain
Of love in this celestrial Fane.
Knowledge, was, indeed, the key,
To unveil the low divine of mystery.

CHAPTER XLIV.

Liberty.

"Few thousand years have rolled away,
Still am basking in the light of day;
A golden tinge is everywhere—.
It gilds the plains of dark despair;
It rests upon the mountain's crest of woe;
Kindness melts the hoary head of snow;
Its sheen, in the garden of the heart,
O'er flowers of Eden, a heavenly glow impart.
Active in love—'tis a photosphere—
Its rays dispel the pearly tear.
Knowledge is potential—its power refined,
Triumphant in the universe of Mind.
A priestly cloud eclipses e'er the sun;
Will be fierce and strong, till its course is run.
Each encroachment, on your rich domain,
Adds blackness to the cloud of Pain.
Why give the ballot and a place of trust,
To a potentate that crumbles you to dust ?
Any power, that tramples on your laws,
Has no sympathy, with a freeman's cause.
A Pope, that says his sway soars o'er a king,
Or any ruler, has a dragon within his saintly ring.
Rip Van Winkle, has at last awoke, to see
The octopus, trying to crush your Liberty.
His arms extend around the treasury of gold;
And would blast the light of the little fold,
Or public schools. *If Superstition would let your rights
alone,*

You would not care who sat upon its throne.
Many glance o'er the Atlantic Sea—
Wish to gain the prize of greatest liberty.
They come; does their gratitude extend
Loyally, as a friend unto a friend ?
Woman's eloquence, pleading for the slave—
Bigotry wished to drive her to her cave
'Twas then, she heard the clanking of her chain,
Which made her sadly wise, and full of pain.
Slander was upon her track;
In vain, did it drive her back
To slavery—in the stormy days of dark midnight—
First ran for freedom and the right.
She sees, through the nimbus of her soul,
No power should e'er control
Her life, or circumscribe her lines;
No Eden lot midst flowers and vines—
A green house, where no acorns grow;
Where the sturdy oak its power can't know.
The eagle, soaring to her lofty aerie,
Loves her young the same as your canary;
She will be the oracles of all the gods
Of wisdom, truth, where e'er the human trods;
She has no "Jewish Wailing Place,"
To mourn and pray; with a lofty grace
Works her way by power of toil,
Up the steps of Time on science' soil.
"'Tis well to have a burnished name,"
A servant girl remarked, while polishing the same.
'Tis by this consecrated shield—
Will enhance the glories of her field.
Francois de Saintonges, was hooted in the streets;
She had a school for girls. a curse greets
Her.   Now colleges arise,
Gladly, by human enterprise.

Daughters of Esculapins, inscribe upon the heart,
Genius in their glorious art;

Her wings of Inspiration, grow in power;
·Knowledge is queen, in her fairy bower
Of Eden; home is a flowery spot indeed,
When not shadowed by any gloomy creed.
Unjust laws, are crumbling in her hand;
Justice will in future, reign all o'er this lovely land.
Man, without love is an icy floe;
An unwise woman, is a bank of snow.
Let each combine the two—
Love and wisdom—then harmony will ensue.
Though I'm the Devil, I like the name;
'Twas I, fanned Freedom into fame;
Have worn the mask in great disguise,
The instigator of Eve, to e'er be wise.
My work is to set the captive free;
Christians, fain would kill me—Liberty !
I let the fires that kindled Voltaire's flame—
That blasted for a time his glorious name.

Thomas Paine—believer in one God—
Was condemned where Christians trod;
His inspired pen, at the helm of State,
Gave men hope not to disintegrate.
Valley Forge, saw Freedom take its stand
Firmly, by the magic of his wand—
Wafted in love o'er each devoted head,
A charm the British lion saw with dread.
I, also cheered him on his way,
To break the chains of religious slavery.

'Twas I, inspired Francois de Saintonges,
For woman's higher progress.
Let Miss Bowen, shout for all,
As well as the gifted Ingersoll.

Though I had an ugly sobrequet,
Yet, I usher in the light of day.
Let Freedom forge the chains—
These are golden; 'tis progress it attains

Which lead to higher planes of truth,
Which do not keep you back forsooth.
Liberty, is whispered o'er the hills;
Liberty is the cadence of all the rills;
Her shield is glittering in the north—
'Tis the watchword called forth,
By every songster in the glen;
'Tis " peace on earth, good will to men !"
Under its rule, each soul shall stand erect,
As conscience, law, in mercy shall direct.
Liberty speaks in thunder tones,
From pole to pole, from all the zones,
'Til it vibrates upon the sky—
" *Kindness*, is the key to harmony."

PART SECOND.

THE

NEW GARDEN OF EDEN.

CHAPTER I.

The Books of Moses.

John W. Draper gives his views of the "Books of Moses", beginning on page 218, in his "Conflict between Science and Religion," as follows:

"From the time of Newton to our own time, the divergence of science from the dogmas of the Church has continually increased. The Church declared that the earth is the central and most important body in the universe; that the sun and moon and stars are tributary to it. On these points she was worsted by astronomy. She affirmed that a universal deluge had covered the earth; that the only surviving animals were such as had been saved in the ark.

"In this her error was established by geology. She taught that there was a first man, who, some six or eight thousand years ago, was suddenly created or called into existence in a condition of physical and moral perfection, and from that condition he fell. But anthropology has shown that human beings existed far back in geological time, and in a savage state, but little better than a brute. Many good and well-meaning men have attempted to reconcile the statements of Genesis with the discoveries of science, but it is in vain. The divergence has increased so much, that it has become an absolute opposition. One of the antagonists must give way."

Further on he states that:

"From Assyrian sources, the legends of the creation of the earth and heaven, the Garden of Eden, the making of man from clay, and of woman from one of his ribs; the temptation by the serpent, the naming of animals, the cherubim and the flaming sword, the Deluge and the Ark, the drying up of the waters by the wind, the building of the Tower of Babel and the confusion of tongues, were obtained by Ezra "

This account is taken from the apocryphal books of Esdras. Page 224, he writes:

"Does not the admission that the narrative of the fall in Eden is legendary carry with it the surrender of that most solemn and sacred Christian doctrine, the atonement ? "

Bishop Colenso writes:

"It is clear that the 'Books of Moses' cannot be imputed to the sole authorship of Moses, since they record his death. It is clear that they were not written until many hundred years after that event, since they contain references to facts which did not occur until after the establishment of the government of kings among the Jews. No man may dare to impute them to the inspiration of Almighty God—their inconsistencies, incongruities, contradictions and impossibilities, as exposed by many learned and pious moderns, both German and English, are so great. It is the decision of these critics that Genesis is a narration based upon legends; that Exodus is not historically true; that the whole Pentateuch is unhistorian and non-Mosaic; it contains the most extraordinary contradictions and impossibilities, sufficient to involve the credibility of the whole—imperfections so great and so conspicuous that they would destroy the authenticity of any modern, historical work."

In the words of Rev. Lyman Abbott, pastor of Plymouth Church:

" I do not believe the bible is infallible. I believe that it is an inspired book, but not infallible. We have one infallible book—Euclid's Geometry. The bible is a product of 3000 years' growth."

The Popes of various denominations do not encourage investigation in the mysteries of the bible; hence, plainly shows how unreliable they regard the sermons they deliver with apparent enthusiasm. Figuratively speaking, the members sit demurely in their respective pews, with eyes closed and say "yes," whenever the preacher states that two and two are five. All nod approval for fear of offending the preacher or God! It is by fear that the self-hood is stultified, and mental slavery is the result.

The pastors watch with care lest their followers escape from the illogical fence of their erection, into the world of thought, where science repeats that two and two are four.

The fervid fathers consider scientists and liberalists as enemies to their creeds, and they regard them as culprits before the bar of God and worthy only the penalty to be given to enjoy the fumes of sulphur through all eternity! They have this knowledge existing in the mind that is biased by the superstition taught them in childhood. To such inflammable material of religious thought, the liberal and scientist should be fined and imprisoned for not believing the many stories in the bible. Every time they have power they execute God's wishes most devoutly!

There is a constant unrest among the pastors, and they feed their respective flocks with the spiritual diet that the nation needs God in the Constitution, or it will perish by the sin of infidelity! The glorious Constitution of these United States rolled into existence in the manner that it did, to give science a home of peace, and that liberalism might not eventually be obliged to whisper its sentiments under the shadow of the tree of superstition for fear of being persecuted by loving Christians!

Can any of the denominations trust each the other in power to rule the destinies of this nation? Certainly not. The child Protestantism has the same attributes of its mother—Catholicism. Quebec has recently viewed the jealousy of the two foes to liberty. The religious mob is the dynamite of superstition. If superstition was relegated to oblivion the war-cry of the savage element would cease to terrorize the helpless and peace would reign. Superstition has persecuted, to some extent, under the flag of liberty, but what would have been the fate of this land were Catholics to gain full control? What would be the result if Protestants were invested with political power? History is a warning that Jews, scientists and liberalists are the ones that would suffer by fine, dungeon and the stake, for the sake of opinion.

A tree is known by its fruit. The fruit is not divine when it leaves an immoral effect to persecute even the vilest person that ever existed. In every soul is a spark of divinity; though many are encrusted by pre-natal impressions and wrong teachings, in early youth will become, sometime, a star of great magnitude in the firmament of heaven's great law of existence. Jews and liberals are self-poised in the realm of morals without the aid of Jesus to help them to high positions in spirituality and patriotism. They never were known to take a dollar of public money and appropriate it for advancing their respective fraternities in any way. It is not patriotic; it is decidedly immoral. The Christian's pendulum of their creed, swings majestically from the great curse of "The Garden of Eden" to the opposite extreme of the improbabilities of the atonement.

NOTE—In the words of Henry Ward Beecher:

"Jesus Christ said, 'I will go on earth and die in their stead,' is a doctrine as infernal as if it had come from the bottomless pit.

"Any view that makes God first angry, and then placated, is blasphemous.

"God's brooding love—not God's avenging law, is the doctrine of the bible. God-saving is the doctrine of the bible, and not God-destroying. Hundreds of young preachers swear to preach this blasphemous system, not knowing what they do, and when they wake up and find what they have sworn to preach, they are silent.

"Men are asking, 'What is the new theology?' There isn't any; but men are finding their way back to the old theology—that is all. It is a march backward, not forward.

"It is the renaissance of theology fighting against the Bizantian; the Bizantian will go down and the new light will go up. I have heard men say of me, 'He is preaching a mush of divine benevolence.' I was not. I was simply taking away the barbaric notion of an avenging God. I have been preaching the fatherhood and motherhood of God.

"If we sin we shall in no way escape the penalty. How long it will last I do not know; that it will last forever I do not believe.

"That men are to be made to suffer forever, to have an eternity of endless torment, I shall not believe outside of a lunatic asylum.

"I shall not go to heaven if I must go through that infernal Confession of Faith to which I once subscribed. God forgive my ignorance—I abhor it."

When a preacher is honest and his conscience active, the reaction is terrible to think he was instrumental in distributing false ideas to the members of his congregation. If his disgust is shown by bitter language, it should be regarded in the light of charity.

Did Henry Ward Beecher wish to persecute Col. R. G. Ingersoll when he was invited to reply to Col. Ingersoll's arguments on the popular religions of the day? He refused to deflect the stream of oratory in that direction and the four thousand dollars had no weight to bear him down in the slough of greed. In contradistinction to this brightest light the Church ever produced, how was the famous agnostic used by the headlight of the wing of superstition—Rev. Mr. Talmage? He would, if it had been in his power, dragged him before the tribunal of injustice and sent him to prison as the worst criminal in any penitentiary in the United States! It is sacrilegious, the Christians repeat, to say aught against the bible. The liberalists must not speak in self-defense against any persecution that may be hurled at them. The liberals have their rights for they are more peaceable than religious people who are vindictive in their thoughts and utterances. The liberals never present a petition to Congress to enact a law to take public money and appropriate it for the dissemination of what they believe to be truth. They regard such transactions as usurping rights; that is the same as purloining, which seems very much in the light of crime.

The religionist says, "It is for the glory of God to distribute the money from the treasury for sectarian purposes." Each sect proclaims its right to the money and if divided among all of them, they would quarrel and persecute each other with peculiar zeal, and not long the treasury would be empty and our nation disgraced! God would be glorified, surely!

Our nation has set the example of the white plume of peace, and it is the Jews and liberals that never have blackened the beautiful emblem of human rights. Under the banner of liberty science has flourished as at no time before in the history of nations.

Liberals never would speak as they do, at present, of the crimes of the Churches if they did not seek to crush Liberty beneath the Juggernaut of superstition.

What is meant by superstition? The religion at the present period has been taken from the different pagan beliefs previous to the time of Jesus, and, also, since his time Christianity has engrafted the rites of the pagan ceremonies in their so called Christian religion. The pagans however, were learned in wisdom and in physical science, but the masses were unlearned and greatly superstitious. If the Christians had taken kindly to science and morals instead the worthless superstition of the pagans, not a person would ever have been sacrificed on the altar of persecution.

A lecturer upon spiritual philosophy, in Yucatan, was annoyed by Catholics, who threw rocks at him while returning from his lecture. The Catholics were arrested. What did the lecturer do? Did he wish to gain notoriety as a martyr? The voices told him to release the Catholics!

Was Jesus ever known to throw rocks at any one by way of argumentation? Verily, a tree is known by its fruit.

Scientists are more intelligent than the God of Moses' invention. Science has revealed the fact that the throat of the largest whale is three and one half inches in diameter. This is a conflict between science and the episode about Jonah and the whale.

God did not know that in the regions of space above the earth the employees on the Tower of Babel could not live; so, he came to earth and performed the miracle of making them speak different languages which baffled their scheme from visiting God by the route of the Tower. This was an invention of ignorance, to account for the origin of various languages. No doubt, that they tried to reach heaven in that manner.

Elisha and Elijah were in a secluded place with no one near to witness Elijah's remarkable exit from the earth. He was equipped with a chariot of fire and horses of the same element and a whirlwind was necessary to give the proper momentum to arise from the earth's attraction safely. Why did not God come to Elijah and command him to cease taking such an excursion to his throne? for no one could breathe or have their being until Gabriel should blow his trumpet!

Literature in bible times was prepared to feed the intellect with unwholesome food that was deleterious in the extreme. The most improbable stories were believed; hence the authors invented the menu that was the most popular.

When Church-members conclude to secede from the Church, they are like little children, in respect of not having been accustomed to do their own thinking. Great care must be taken not to fall into other beliefs that are. equally, and, perhaps, more absurd than the dogmas they once cherished as sacred. Sometimes fear drives them back, not being well equipped in knowledge of the contradictions of the bible and its many errors. To such people the Church is a solace, and the pastors like to establish that condition of mind. When they have a desire to persecute another, whether inside or outside of the Church, is an indication they are far from living near the God they profess to adore. A vindictive spirit is not the sign of divinity that they think they possess. Vindictiveness thinks it has the prerogative to destroy the rights and privileges of others in regard to life, liberty and the pursuit of happiness.

The enthusiasts in the Church dislike the last innovation into their biblical arena for Evolution strikes at the root of their decaying tree with a force that is destined to annihilate, forever, its time-honored propoitions. The myth of the "Garden of Eden" being the foundation of the tenets of the Church, the sooner the truth is known the better for mankind. Evolution will never recede, but walks majestically to the altar and plants the banner of victory firmly in the rock of truth, and the tree falls, never more to be resuscitated and resume its former activity in supplying bitter fruit for humanity.

Scientific truth is spreading rapidly and the Church is alarmed at the infidel Science, but modestly claim to be on warlike terms with Infidelity!

Nature's laws move on in one grand system of harmony, without a flaw in its machinery. It is reasonable to suppose that if the bible was written by the dictation of a supreme ruler of the universe, that the inspirations would surpass all that could be composed by the most talented mortal. It would be chaste, pure, exalted in sentiment and its influence angelic, godlike.

The bible was a wonderful production, in the ages of credulity and ignorance. A new work, written at the present time, would be relegated to oblivion that contained like errors and superstition. This fact is a sure indication that humanity has progressed out of its crude condition, and when it bids adieu, forever, to the bible as a holy book, it will be correspondingly pure and humane.

The books claimed to be written by Moses, contain another view of the woman question but little understood by ladies that belong to the various Churches. The pastors failed to inform them that in the first chapter woman enjoys the prerogative of being on equal terms with man. Adam and Eve were endowed by the great Jehovah with the crowns as king and queen over their immense possessions which was the whole earth. Together they held the power to rule over every living thing. Adam and Eve must have been very happy in their marriage relation. Marriage was not a failure in that case, for there existed no divinity whip in the word "obey" to make Eve unhappy and to stultify the good qualities that Adam possessed.

God created the pair, man and woman, and said his work was "good." He told no untruth in that respect, in being obliged to say that he made a decided failure in his enterprise, and it was justice to punish his poor work in a style worthy of one holding such a high position in the universe!

In chapter first, there existed no tree that was called "Knowledge," consequently, no satan visited their territory who had conversational powers.

It is a plain, matter-of-fact story, altogether too tame to give as a text in a sensational sermon.

The complete subjugation of womankind was a theme dwelt upon with so much zeal that woman has bowed submissively to the rod they believed was sanctioned by the Lord.

Woman's rights would have been popular, ages ago, if that tradition of the Garden of Eden had been worded for women to hold the power to rule man, instead of man enslaving women, he would strike for his rights very quickly. Peradventure, he would obtain his dues in a much shorter period of time than fifty years!

The Christian lady believes what little rights she has is far superior to the women that lived before the Christian era. Samuel Johnson's researches into oriental religions states that:

"Germany and Rome believed woman was as fit to bear the rod of Empire as man. They established the open doctrine that, in domestic, social and civil life, the woman was the equal of the man. The common law of England put woman to death for crimes which a clergyman could commit without fear of punishment, and for which the severest punishment to a man was branding."

The history of different countries in ancient times places woman on perfectly equal terms with man, showing how the tradition of woman's fall did not come from the most enlightened nations, but from some semi-savage people we might call barbarians. The common law of Christian England lowered her standard under which cruelty has been enacted upon the stage of life that is a disgrace to any kingdom or republic.

The editor of the "Banner of Light" writes that:—

"Woman, deprived of the right to her own offspring; woman, forbidden to hold or dispose of property; woman, made the physical slave of her husband, and a brutal husband's lusts; woman, with her wrists manacled, and following the back of her "lord's" chariot. It is not Christianity that has improved this harsh cruelty in any part; it is the advancement of the human mind; the progress of physical and social science; the culture of the intellect, and the recognition of an increasing necessity. And it is upon these higher, larger, and better views that her further emancipation is to proceed."

What is Col. Ingersoll's opinion on such an important theme as the woman question? He says:

"Now, then, my friends, while men have been the slaves of men, women have been the slaves of slaves. They have not even had half of the rights that have been given to men. Oh, I do hate a man who thinks he is the head of the family. During all these ages, woman, I say, was a slave of man, and to a certain extent, is to-day. How many men I have heard say that they were superior to any woman; they knew more than any woman; and when we talk about woman having voice in the Government, every body says, "No." I say she has the same right to take a part in the Government, if she desires, as I have."

Those men who made such generous remarks about their capabilities as being superior to any woman (think of that assertion), if they knew how they had fallen in the great man's estimation, would blush with shame at their egotism.

The Navajoes believe that God is a white woman that

comes to them down the mountain side. The effect of this belief is, that woman is not annoyed by their natural protectors endeavoring in every way that greed suggests to bankrupt her financially. Women among the Navajoes are entrusted with property as though she was possessed with honesty and common sense. Civilization rises or falls in proportion as woman is used with respect or disrespect. A religious belief can make her a slave or exalt her. If it has the word "obey" in the marriage ceremony it degrades her. That is a silent manner in which the pastor gives the whip to the man which says in plain words to chastise your wife when she is striking for justice! This deleterious belief is so firmly rooted in the mind of some devotees, in a certain denomination, that the women expect to be literally whipped, occasionally, for it is God's will! The priesthood are responsible for this injustice.

The effect of the unkind word flashes along the electric wires of the nerves with tremendous power, creating sad havoc with life's delicate machinery, which is instrumental in causing disease to take the place of health, which eventually overpowers the victim and woman sinks at the feet of her husband—who has murdered her by law; by the divinity of the whip and by the command of the God of the bible!

Many people have believed for a long time that grief has a deleterious effect upon the system, and, recently, this fact has been demonstrated by science.

One of our leading dailies, printed in San Francisco, contains this news:

"The Government is about to start a psycho-physical laboratory for research, to study poisons produced by emotions, by analyzing the perspiration of different people. Prof. Elmer Gates has been appointed to take charge of it. It deals with matters which hitherto have been deemed beyond reach of investigation.

Among other things, it has discovered that bad and unpleasant feelings create harmful chemical products in the body which are physically injurious. Good, pleasant, benevolent and cheerful feelings create beneficial chemical products which are physically healthful. These products may be obtained by chemical analysis in the perspiration of the individual. Professor Gates has discovered more than forty of the bad and as many of the good."

Further on this interesting article, says:

"Of all the chemical products of emotions, that of guilt is the worst. If a small quantity of the perspiration of a person suffering from feelings of that kind be placed in a glass tube and exposed to contact with selenic acid, it will turn pink. Accordingly, pink would appear to be the characteristic color of wrong-doing. How, appropriate, then, that the wicked person should blush of his evil deeds. It is a question whether he does so, very often, however."

He writes that this science is not visionary but is based on facts. Again:

"To sum up, it is found that for each bad emotion there is a corresponding chemical change in the tissues of the body which is life-depressing and poisonous. Contrari-wise, every good emotion makes a life-promoting change. Thus, it follows, that it pays to be good and to do good, for one's own sake. A noble and generous action blesses the doer as well as the beneficiary."

It has been demonstrated that woman's pathway has been obstructed by the whip; the block and the chains are symbols of slavery. She has found that man has no divine right to rule.

Whenever a man wishes his liberty he never ceases trying until his object is obtained. If it is manly for a man to strike for his rights it is equally womanly for woman to cross the icy river into the territory of freedom. If strength of mind is a noble quality in man, it certainly should grace a woman's intellect with the same degree of perfection. Strength of mind, combined with mercy, is a decided evolution from nonentity. The mussulman brought his wife with him to the World's Fair, that possessed the most strength, intellectually, hence, more companionable and brilliant.

Strength of mind signifies power to carry out small and great enterprises successfully.

Strength of mind creates stability in morals and maintains principles against persecution.

Strength of mind instead of creating discord at home and in society, can, by its discriminating power and a high sense of justice, calm the disturbing elements far more than a weak and vacillating person who lacks wisdom and executive abilities.

A Man's Word for Woman.

BY T. L. HARRIS.

By this we hold: No man is wholly great,
    Or wise, or just, or good,
Who will not dare his all to *reinstate*
    Earth's trampled womanhood.

No Seer sees truly, save as he discerns
    Her crowned, co-equal right;
No lover loves divinely, till he burns
    Against her foes to fight.

That Church is fallen, proue as Lucifer,
  God's bolts that hath not hurled
Against the tyrants who have outraged her,
  The Priestess of the world.

That Press, whose minions, slavish and unjust,
  Bid her in fetters die,
Toils, in the base behalf of Pride and Lust,
  To consecrate a lie.

" *Once* it was Christ, whom Judas with a kiss
  Betrayed," the Spirit saith :
" But now, 'tis Woman's heart inspired by His,
  That man consigns to death."

Each village hath its martyrs—every street
  Some house that is a hell ;
Some woman's heart, celestial, pure and sweet
  Breaks with each passing bell.

There are deep wrongs, too infinite for words,
  Man dare not have revealed ;
And, in our midst, insane, barbaric hordes,
  Who make the Law their shield.

Rise, then, oh WOMAN ! grasp the mighty pen,
  By Inspirations driven ;
Scatter the sophistries of cruel men,
  With voices fresh from Heaven.

Man, smiting thee, moves on from war to war ;
  All rights with thine decease,
Rise, 'throned with Christ, in his pure morning star,
  And charm the world to Peace.

CHAPTER II.
Maledictions.

To the liberal who has outgrown aught that is savage
in his nature, has arisen above the shadow of curses such

as exists in the spirit of the Church at the present time, and considers them too low in the scale of civilization to utter or write about, only under the pressure of necessity.

When maledictions have entirely vanished from the creeds, then will earth be clothed with flowers of affection and no clashing of steel be heard for the sake of opinion, to wither the beautiful emblems of peace. God cursed the devil, Adam, Eve and the ground. What effect has cursing the ground left upon mankind? This is one: A woman has lost an infant by death; could not bury her child in consecrated soil in a graveyard for the reason, the little innocent baby had not been baptized! The consequence was, she left the church forever.

Another effect is given in the San Diego, Cal. paper:

How They Carried the Sacred Timbers.

"The priests who built the old San Diego Mission in 1769 and thereabouts, had to go a long distance inland for the roof timbers to support the heavy tiles made of adobe. From the old woman now living at Josepha Peters, near San Luis Rey, and whom we believe to be at least 124 years of age, Mr. W. B. Couts learned that the timbers for the Mission came from Smith's Mountain, at least sixty miles inland from this city. The old lady says that after the timbers had all been nicely hewed and prepared, and blessed by the priests on the mountain, on a certain day a vast number of the stoutest Indians were collected and stationed in relays of about a mile apart, all the way from the summit of the mountain to the foundations of the Mission buildings in the valley near this city.

At a given signal the timbers were blessed by the assembled priests on the mountain, and were then hoisted on the shoulders of the Indians, and were thus carried to the first relays and changed to their shoulders, and so on, all the way to San Diego, without touching the ground; it was considered a sacrilege to have one of them touch the ground from the time of starting till it arrived at its final destination in the Church."

If the priests had blessed the whole earth, then their journey down the mountain would have been with less trouble.

Think how mankind are every day obliged to walk upon ground that is held under ban, as a convict that has committed unpardonable sin ! The priesthood should be anxious to leave this unholy planet and devise some way to go to heaven as Elijah did, in fine style.

In a well-regulated, liberal family, a curse is never heard to darken the moral atmosphere with its blighting influence. To wish a liberal should reside in hades is one great source of crime.

Does Divinity visit an altar when the atmosphere vibrates with the following waves of inharmony in regard to human rights? They are :

"A man who has been excommunicated by the Pope may be killed anywhere."—BUSSAMBAUM

"We are to take with unquestionable docility whatever instruction the Church gives us."—["Catholic World."

"Our Church is God's Church, and not accountable either to state or country."—POPE PIUS IX.

"The freedom of thinking is simply nonsense."—MGR. SEGUR.

"There is, ere long, to be a State religion in this country, and that State religion is to be Roman Catholic."—FATHER HECKER.

Said Castelar, in his speech in Catholic Spain, before a Catholic Cortes in 1869 :

"There is not a single progressive principle that has

not been cursed by the Catholic Church. This is true of England and Germany, as well as of Catholic countries. The Church cursed the French Revolution, the Belgian Constitution, and the Italian Independence; nevertheless, all these principles have been enrolled in spite of it. Not a Constitution has been born, not a single progress made, not a solitary reform effected, which has not been under the terrible anathemas of the Church."

Here are a few of many instances where the Pope's blessings do not seem to bless:

"This Pope gave his blessing to Maximilian, as Emperor of Mexico, and in a short time thereafter, he, the blessed one, was shot to death at Queretaro.

"His Empress, Carlotta, was received with great consideration in Rome, where she was granted his benediction by the Pope in person, but before she left the Vatican she was hopelessly insane.

"Isabella II of Spain, was showered with Papal blessings, and inside a month after the imposing ceremony, she was dethroned. For "a pious daughter of the Church" none received more frequent blessings than the Empress Eugenia, and it is claimed, with considerable force, that she, at the request of the Jesuits, fomented the war which left her without a throne and an exile in England. An English steamer, the Santa Maria, having on board Sisters of Charity, en route for Montevideo, which, in 1870, was blessed by the Holy Father, burnt to the water's edge, and all on board perished. All on account of the Pope's benedictions."

CHAPTER III.

Sunday Law.

Did Jesus, while on earth, circulate a petition to fasten ecclesiastical chains on the people? Was it his mission to invent a pillory for the benefit of his followers who were inclined to have an individuality of their own? If such methods had actuated his motives the multitude never would follow him with love and gratitude.

He boldly proclaimed that the "Sabbath was made for man and not man for the Sabbath."

He saw, with regret, the cruel law of Moses being enforced around him, and he undertook the herculean task to stay the mighty flood of destruction as it swept down through the ages giving moral disease to those hurling stones and death to the innocent—who had perpetrated no crime whatever.

Knowing the status of the barbaric age in which he lived, saw with prophetic eye that his life would be sacrificed, but rather than have future generations persecuted, pursued his own course for the benefit of the human race.

By his clashing with the laws of Moses he was at war with the fanatical priesthood. They delighted in the screeches of persecution that came from the victims of the Mosaic Inquisition. Jesus looked with indignation at the long-faced, hypocritcal priests, and knew how to attract the masses. The new dispensation of the law of love was greeted with enthusiasm. They listened with rapture when he taught them the golden rule in the great cathedral of nature. The songsters echoed the inspired words with harmonious strains in the dome of this sacred Church. The multitude loved him for his deeds of mercy which were the key to his heart. It would have been an easy task for him to be popular with the society in his time. If he had been a hypocrite his name would have faded in the midnight of selfishness and nonentity.

After his death his followers met together by force of habit, no doubt, on the seventh day of the week, for communion of some kind and when they were numerous, sufficient for the pagans to persecute them, Constantine saw the contending forces in his dominion, and it was policy to give his royal sanction for the Christians to change their time of communion from the seventh to the first day of the week. Sunday, the great day for sun-worshippers, was the day for pagans and Christians to worship together in peace. It is easy to repeat at the present era that Sunday is God's holy day! Jesus regarded all days holy, but the famous murderer by the name of Constantine has completely eclipsed the brilliant career of the great reformer Jesus!

Jesus completely annihilated the austerity of the old Sabbath custom of cruelty. The question arises where and when did the influence of the bible return to give gloom and death to the people again?

Did Constantine persecute any one for working on the pagan Sunday? It is not so recorded, but to his honor his decree was to work to save crops if necessary on Sunday.

Coming down the stream of time to the reign of Queen Elizabeth, although the death penalty was instituted for many innocent deeds, still no one was punished for working on Sunday. On the contrary, it was a law to save crops on Sunday if necessary, for God would be displeased if they were left to perish. Mark this, when a sect claims to be exceedingly pure, distrust it. There was a sect that were called Noncomformists.

The Nonconformists were called Puritans in derision, no doubt, at first. They were so pure they also persecuted the helpless at the first opportunity.

The Puritans made Sunday hideous with their frowns. The law of Moses was revived and the American Inquisition was a disgrace to purity. When ministers desire the good old Puritan days to return it means persecution.

The framers of the Constitution of the United States had witnessed the object lesson of the union of Church and State to its fullest perfection, and, therefore, they saw the necessity of eliminating the Church from the State for the lofty purpose that persecution might cease under the glorious flag of equal rights for all to worship according to the dictates of conscience, so long as the rights of each are respected.

Now we will see what Science has to reveal upon the Sabbath question:

SCIENCE AND SUNDAY.

"The thing is done and science did it. The Sunday grievance in all its multifarious wickedness is settled at last. Those who insist upon our observing a commandment that Jesus and Paul left out whenever they repeated the Sinatic commandments, and they who believe the Sabbath is not an observance required of Christians at all—can both be at rest, each contented, each performing all that is required of him. The manner in which this beautiful effort of science smoothes away existing difficulties, and enables the Sabbath lion and the anti-Sabbath lamb to lie down in peace together, is thus explained. When circumnavigation of the globe became as common as life insurance agents, oaths of a ward politician, and declarations of honesty in a

United States Senator's speech, it was found necessary to take some measures to calm the minds of sea-faring men, who on arriving home after having put a belt around this mundame sphere of ours, felt outraged because their views of the day of the week on which they landed were not accepted by the denizens of terra firma. Conscientious Connecticut captains, who had voyaged from New York to San Francisco, and thence home again by the Cape of Good Hope, would sometimes reach home on what they knew by their reckonings was Saturday, and would find their friends in the very midst of Sunday; while wicked New York captains, who had circumnavigated the globe in the opposite direction, would land on what they believed Sunday morning, and would have their anticipations of a Sabbath-day spree dashed by being told that it was Saturday. So much discontent was caused by this state of things that maritime nations finally fixed upon a meridian in the Pacific ocean as the precise point where vessels bound east or west should lose or gain a day. Since this plan was adopted the circumnavigating mariner returns home, not to unprofitable disputations, but at peace with the calender and his fellow-men. There is no special reason why a spot in the Pacific should be taken for the purpose mentioned. A government may appoint any other meridian if it so choose."

If we are to take the one running down the San Francisco Bay, there would then be a difference of twenty-four hours between San Francisco and Oakland. Monday morning in San Francisco would be Tuesday morning in Oakland, and the people who started from Oakland at 12 o'clock on Wednesday would arrive at the foot of Market street at 20 minutes past 12 on Tuesday, 23 hours and 40 minutes before they started. No one can doubt the soundness of this reasoning without striking a blow at all faith in mathematics and astronomy, and we can only wonder that its application to the Sunday question was not long since proposed.

Now if it were thus practicable for San Franciscans to gain an entire day by crossing the bay, what right would Church people have to find fault with Sunday excursions to Oakland? We could leave here on Sunday and have a good time in Oakland, or that vicinity, without shocking religious nerves by Sabbath-breaking. We could have Monday "off" in Oakland and get back here Sunday night without losing a day, and at the same time be at peace with the law and the fourth commandment. If you don't understand this thing as thoroughly as you feel that you should on religious principles, read Jules Verne in "Round the World in 80 Days."

J. M. Peebles writes as follows:

"THE LOST DAY.

"Since sailing upon the Pacific westward, the question has been sprung, 'Where does day begin?' The general answer was, 'Here—there—or at that place where the sunbeams first strike the earth during the twenty-four hours.' The geographical and nautical answer is, 'Day begins at the degree of longitude 180 east or west'. Every schoolboy knows that traveling round the world from east to west a day is literally lost, and for the reason that there is a difference of one hour for every fifteen degrees of longtitude in each day. Accordingly, journeying westward, a certain length of time is added to each day; and making the world's circuit—as many are doing at present—would amount to an entire day. This is a puzzler to strict observers of 'Sabbath-days.' When crossing the meridian 180, before reaching Auckland, New Zealand, our captain dropped from his reckonings the day we had lost—and Sunday was this very lost day! How queer! going to bed Saturday night, and getting up on Monday morning!

"Round the world tourists crossing the Pacific en route for Japan, on arriving at the 180 degree of longitude, drop a day from their calender. The returning ship adds a day to its reckoning. It happened to the Rev. Dr. Field crossing this meridian on the 18th of June, which fell on Sunday, to enjoy two successive Sundays in mid-ocean, one of which was the Sunday of Asia, the other that of America and Europe. The reverend chronicler sadly records the fact that many of his fellow voyagers, in their perplexity as to which day ought to be observed, failed to keep either day, and so, instead of gaining two Sundays, lost the one which was theirs by right."

The learned Brahmin dashed the microscope upon the floor, for he did not wish his followers' faith shaken in transmigration of souls. If it was honorable for Christians to deceive in regard to longitude and time, then it is honorable for the Brahmin to teach the transmigration of souls in his religion.

ASTROLOGY AND THE HEBREWS.

"It is well known to scholars who have investigated the subject, that the week of seven days had its origin in astrology, which was practiced in the east at a very early date. The division of time into periods of seven days can be traced to Egypt, but it probably came from Chaldea where astrology seems to have originated.

The seven days of the week bear the names of the seven planets, counting the sun and moon, or of the deities supposed to preside over them, over which the planets were supposed to bear rule, in the following order: Sunday, the sun; Monday, the moon; Tuesday, Mars; Wednesday, Mercury; Thursday, Jupiter; Friday, Venus; Saturday, Saturn.

The singular order observed in the arrangement of the planets is also accounted for by the astrological system of the ancients.   The Egyptian astrologers termed Saturn the "greater infortune," and as he ruled Saturday it was popularly considered unpropitious to commence any undertaking on that day, and from this probably originated the custom of resting on the seventh day.

The names of the days of the week in the Latin, in French, and most of the Oriental languages, were directly derived from the ruling planets, and in the order given above.   An English author who has been investigating this subject, shows that a similar connection between the week and the planets exists in the Hebrew, which is not surprising as the Hebrews derived many of their customs from the ancient Egyptians."—[Ex.

Science is a great iconoclast and it is only a question of time when Sunday will cease to be regarded as God's holy day.

The clergy of Minneapolis have made themselves conspicuous in their ignorance by pledging themselves to withhold all patronage from the Sunday newspaper, believing that the Sunday newspaper is the head and front of all offending.

It is that kind of fanatics that have persecuted many in the United States, liberals and Seventh Day Adventists who were working on Sunday and doing nobody any harm.   In Dec. 30th, 1889, Jews in Lowell, Mass., were arrested for dancing, and fined for the reason the music disturbed the puritans on the Lord's Holy Day. The most agitation in regard to persecution of persons for working on Sunday has been in Kansas and Tennessee.   Here is a newspaper account of the affair:

"Those who are demanding a Sunday law find they have no scripture to present for Sunday keeping, so they want to bolster up their cause with a civil enactment. Adventists are now in jail in both Kansas and Tennessee for working on Sunday, and they are not 'driven to it by the greed of corporations' either. One man is lying in jail with felons for gathering over ripe fruit from his own orchard on Sunday. Collections were taken up in our churches last week for the families of brethren who are in Tennessee jails, and in consequence their families are suffering. I think we need a law to protect Adventists from the persecution of their neighbors quite as much as a Sunday law to protect people from the rapacity of corporations."

The above facts occurred in 1886.

The United States Supreme Court had not passed upon the constitutionality of the Sunday law and it was to decide on this question in the case of Mr. King, but ere the time arrived Mr. King died, no doubt, prematurely by the cruelty of the American Christian Inquisition. Mr. King was a Seventh Day Adventist; was indicted for cultivating his corn on Sunday on his own premises. He was arraigned before a justice of the peace and fined. Afterwards he was indicted by the Grand Jury for the same offense and was convicted and fined $75. His case was appealed to the Supreme Court, and his conviction was there affirmed. There were many having great interest in this case when it was decided to take it to the United States Supreme Court, but his death was a shock to the thousands who knew him to be another martyr that has fallen a victim in the flames of superstition.

Tennesse is religious. It has quite a perfect system of the union of Church and State. The whipping post is revived and the criminals are whipped in true puritanic style. It is reported that women in the prisons are stripped to the waist and whipped on the bare back.

Yes, Tennessee is grandly pious.. It must have men in office that believe in future rewards and punishments.

California has no Sunday law. Bigotry has tried to fasten such a law upon the State, but the State to the present time has too much humanity to allow its subjects to wear the chains of religious slavery. California owes its freedom on Sunday greatly to two liberals who have worked diligently to establish liberal ideas all along the Pacific Coast. One is Dr. J. L. York, who was a preacher for twenty years and by the light of reason bade adieu to superstition and became an Ingersoll of the Coast, in lecturing on reform subjects. At one time he was Senator in the legislature in Sacramento.

The other, Samuel P. Putnam, a liberal lecturer, and whenever he is needed to talk to a committee at the Capitol, he is there to advocate the cause of humanity by his logic and his arguments which are effective.

Would that men of their ability could help in all the States to establish what our forefathers intended, a home of liberty for all.

Only three States in all this broad domain that has no Sunday Law. These are California, Idaho and Wyoming.

Liberal lecturers do not work in the field of Reform for self-glory or to earn merely a living. They see danger all along the horizon of our land and they seek to avoid the possibility of a fearful crisis that may ensue if people are not firm in eternal vigilance which seems to be the price of liberty so long as superstition is as powerful as at present. Behold the danger in the contest in 1888 when large delegations from numerous and powerful Christian organizations sought to overwhelm the United States Congress with their speeches and petitions that represented 14,000,000 Christians !

The object of the celebrated Blair bill, was to secure the Lord's day as a day of rest and to promote its observance as a day of public worship ! Cardinal Gibbon's letter added weight, also, to the respectability of the influence of the august assembly.

Among those who favored toleration was the great Senator from New Hampshire who failed in his most Christian object. Perhaps the words of the opponents to his bill reverberated through the halls with a pathos that could not be resisted when they repeated that "Congress shall make no law respecting the establishment of religion or prohibiting the free exercise thereof."

Much misery might have been avoided had there been in the Constitution a clause to the same effect that no State could interfere with the rights of conscience in respect to religion or prohibit the free exercise thereof. It has been a blot upon our nation that is supposed to give liberty to all, that so many people have been fined, and inmates of the penitentiaries along with the lowest criminals in those institutions. If our nation continues to be apathetic, at no distant time all States will be as religious as Delaware and Tennessee.

Many well-meaning Christians may be likened to dead fish that float along with the popular current, and it is too much exercise for the mind to think for themselves to swim with the live fish up the stream of time. They are not aware the great benefit of the protection of our

Constitution, for it answers as a check to a considerable degree to the encroachments of the demands of fanatics. To sign a petition that lessens liberty, signs their own death warrant. Catholicism would assert its claims and either Protestantism or Catholicism would have to yield. The prospect is not brilliant, to institute laws for the use of racks, wheels, boot, thumb-screws, burning at the stake, etc., etc., to reappear to decorate our statute books with death warrants of the brightest intellects of our land.

Women are taking an active part in reforming the Constitution, and the next item will be the ideas of a large class that have outgrown the narrow ideas that Bigotry always gives

THE RIGHTS OF WOMEN.

The following is an excerpt from a speech delivered by Elizabeth Cady Stanton, President of the National American Woman Suffrage Association, in Washington City on the 18th of last February:

"We might get some agitation by trying a new field for our labors, demanding equality for woman in the Church. As women are the chief supporters of the Church, get up all the fairs and donation parties, do all the begging to build Churches, support missionaries and theological seminaries, many of them making large bequests to these various institutions, one would think the time had fully come for woman to demand of the same equal recognition she demands of the State. She should assume her right and duty to take part in the revision of bibles, prayerbooks and creeds; to vote on all questions of business, and to fill the offices of deacon, elder, Sunday school superintendent, pastor and bishop, and have the right to sit and vote as delegate in all ecclesiastical conventions, synods and assemblies, that thus our religion may no longer reflect only the masculine element in humanity, and that woman—the mother of the race—may be honored as she must be before we can have a happy home, a rational religion and an enduring government.

"If educated women had exerted any enlightened influence on the religious thought of the world, leading men in the nineteenth century would not stand debating the damnation of infants at this hour, harrowing up the souls of pale mothers, sorrowing over the loss of their first born. Men not endowed with the maternal instinct may pass unscathed through the ordeal of such a discussion, but alas, for the young mothers all over this land who read these atrocious sentiments in cold type, as they decorate with flowers the little graves of their loved ones! Our insane asylums are full of susceptible, imaginative young women, whose reason has been dethroned by these religious superstitions. Surely the mother-love, once set free from old creeds and dogmas, must bring to humanity new light and hope, both for this world and the world to come.

"As women are taking an active part in pressing on the consideration of Congress many narrow sectarian measures, such as more rigid Sunday laws, to stop travel and the distribution of the mail on that day, and to introduce the name of God into the constitution—as this action on the part of some woman is used as an argument for the disfranchisement of all, I hope this convention will declare that the Woman's Suffrage Association is opposed to all union of Church and State, and pledges, itself as far as possible, to maintain the secular nature of our government. As Sunday is the only day the laboring men can escape from the cities, to stop the street cars, omnibuses and railroads would, indeed, be a lamentable exercise of arbitrary authority. No, no, the duty of the State is to protect those who do the work of the world in the largest liberty, and instead of shutting them up in their gloomy tenement houses on Sunday, we should open wide the parks, horticultural gardens, the museums, the libraries, the galleries of art, and the music halls where they can listen to the divine melodies of the great masters. All these are questions of legislation, and what influence women will exert as voters is already being canvassed; hence the importance of this association expressing its opinions on all questions on which woman's social, civil, religious and political rights are involved.

"Consider the thousands of women with babies in their arms, year after year, who have no change to the dull routine of their lives, except on Sunday when their husbands can go with them on some little excursion by land or sea, suddenly compelled to stay at home by the passage of a rigid Sunday law, secured by the votes of those who can drive about at pleasure in their own carriages, and go wherever they may desire."

THE FATHER JASPERS.

"The 'Pioneer Press' has been fairly deluged with communications in answer to the recent concerted attacks made by Minneapolis clergymen on the Sunday newspapers. Most of these are of a highly satirical character, and hardly do justice to the motives of the gentlemen of the cloth. We will not have the sincerity of our clerical censors impeached or their ancient and time-honored notions treated with disrespectful levity. The man, who, in this day and generation, thinks it sinful to read a Sunday newspaper is an interesting relic of an order of things which is as distinctly obsolete in the system of modern thought and as distinctly incompatible with the exigencies of modern social life as the man who still believes in witchcraft or in the divine right of kings. He would, if he could, make Sunday so uncomfortable for Christians that before long there would be very few Christians left to keep him company in his gloomy isolation from the active and cheerful world, which needs and will have a cheerful and comfortable Sunday. The Sunday newspaper is the natural and inevitable outgrowth of modern social life. It came as the Sunday street car has come—in response to an imperative public need; and it has come to stay. The question of its legitimacy or of its necessity is as absolutely settled for all time to come as the question of the revolution of the earth on its axis. And the Father Jaspers who keep on proclaiming from their pulpits with the ancient authorities of the church that 'the sun do move' command about as much deference from the great body of public opinion as their picturesque Virginia prototype."

The following episode is an instance of persecution in the good old days of Puritanism :

"Capt. St. Leo, commander of a warship then in Boston Harbor, being apprehended for walking on the Lord's Day, was sentenced by a justice of the peace to pay a fine, and on refusing to pay had to sit in the stocks an hour during the day. While in the stocks the good people supplied him with much good advice as to his future conduct on the Sabbath day. After his release, the captain expressed great regret for his past transgressions, and declared to them that he was in future resolved to lead a new life. The saints of Boston were, of course, delighted at his sudden reformation, and in order that the captain might still further profit by their good counsel, many of them invited him to dinner. The captain proved to be a most zealous convert. He attended prayer-meeting and showed every outward sign of grace. At length he was obliged to put to sea, and before the day of departure invited many of the spiritual advisers to dinner aboard the vessel, which lay ready in Nantasket Roads. A capital dinner was provided, at which many bottles were drained to the captain's health. When the after-dinner harmony was at its height a body of sailors burst into the cabin and seized the guests. They were dragged on deck, tied to a grating, and the boatswain and his assistants administered the law of Moses in a most energetic manner, the captain, meantime, assuring them that the mortification of the flesh tended to the saving of the soul, were bundled into their boat and the captain immediately set sail."

The Whipping post was once established as a law in Nevada. The citizens of the Silver State pulled them up, much to their honor, as loving humanity more, and superstition less, than in the State of Delaware.

The screeches of the victims of brutality is not known to echo among the silver crested mountains of this progressive State. Nevada has its faults, but it has not degenerated to the "Dark Ages," as yet, and it is to be hoped the liberty-loving people will, at no distant day, sweep away every unjust law from the statute books, and give more extended rights to every citizen, whether man or woman.

The Church is empowered with no divine right to dictate about any day of the week to be set apart for religious purposes and compel people to go to Church by blockading the right of way to walk or ride in the sunshine of happiness and freedom.

The "Century" says :

"America has three bulwarks of liberty—a free ballot, a free school, and a free Sunday—and neither domestic treachery nor foreign impudence should be permitted to break them down."

CHAPTER IV.

The Pedigree of Christianity.

Writing of the amalgamation of Christianity and Paganism, Draper has many comparisons, but will give a few which are as follows :

"Olympus was restored, but the divinities passed under other names. The more powerful provinces insisted on the adoption of their time-honored conceptions. Views of the trinity, in accordance with Egyptian traditions, were established.

"The well-known effigy of the goddess Isis, with the infant Horus in her arms, has descended to our days in the beautiful, artistic creations of the Madonna and child.

"When it was announced to the Ephesians that the Council of that place, headed by Cyril, had decreed that the Virgin should be called the Mother of God, with tears of joy they embraced the knees of their bishop; it was the old instinct peeping out; their ancestors would have done the same for Diana. Let us pause here, a moment, and see, in anticipation, to what a depth of intellectual degradation this policy of paganization eventually led. Heathen rites were adopted, a pompous and splendid ritual, gorgeous robes, mitres, tiaras, wax-tapers, processional services, lustrations, gold and silver vases, were introduced. The Roman lituus, the chief ensign of the augurs, became the crozier.

"Fasting became the grand means of repelling the devil and appeasing God; celibacy the greatest of the virtues. The virtues of consecrated water were upheld; images and relics were introduced into the Churches, and worshiped after the fashion of the heathen gods. It was given out that prodigies and miracles were to be seen in certain places, as in heathen times. There was a multiplication of temples, altars and penitential garments. The worship of images, of fragments of the cross, or bones, nails, and other relics; a true fetich worship, was cultivated.

"Two arguments were relied on for the authenticity of those objects—the authority of the Church, and the working of miracles. Even the worn-out clothing of the saints, and the earth of their graves were venerated. From Palestine were brought what were affirmed to be

the skeletons of St. Mark and St. James, and other ancient worthies. Then came the mystery of transub-
stantiation or the conversion of bread and wine by the
priest into the flesh and blood of Christ.

"As centuries passed, the paganism became more
complete. Festivals sacred to the memory of the lance
with which the Saviour's side was pierced, the nails that
fastened him to the cross, and the crown of thorns, were
instituted. Though there were several abbeys that
possessed this last peerless relic, no one dared to say that
it was impossible they could all be authentic."

Bishop Newton on the paganism of Christianity
writes :

"The burning of incense or perfumes on several altars
at one and the same time, the sprinkling of holy water,
or a mixture of salt and water, at going into and coming out of places of public worship; the lighting up
of a great number of lamps and wax candles in broad
daylight before altars and statues; the hanging up of
votive offerings and rich presents as attestations of so
many miraculous cures and deliverances from diseases
and dangers; the canonization or deification of deceased
worthies; the consecrating and bowing down to images;
the carrying of images and relics in pompous procession,
with numerous lights, and with music and singing; flag-
ellations at solemn seasons under notion of penance; the
shaving of priests, or the tonsure, as it is called, on the
crown of the heads—all these and many more rites and
ceremonies are equally parts of pagan and popish worship."

We will pass from the uniformity of heathen and
Christian Rome and trace some beliefs to Egypt as
adopted by the Jews.

D. M. Bennett writes:

"A hereditary priesthood with divine rights; the
phrase, 'I am that I am'; white linen robes of the

priests; the rich temple and holy of holies; the cherubim with extended wings; urim and thummim as symbolical jewels; branched candlesticks; animal sacrifice to deity; the rule of the priesthood; a veritable theocracy; prayer to affect deity; the monotheistic idea."

WHAT CHRISTIANITY BORROWED FROM EGYPT.

"Doctrine of the trinity; belief in a being half man and half god; the cross as a religious symbol; the belief of an evil being antagonistic to God; belief in a local heaven and hell; the Christmas festival; the Candlemas festival; a keeper of the keys of heaven; the practice of holy pilgrimages; linen surplices worn by priests; shaving the heads of priests; the priesthood claiming divine knowledge; the resurrection of the body."

In the words of D. B. Bennett we have:

"Father Huc, when he went to Asia, as a missionary, declared that the devil had preceded him and established the Christian religion. Buddhism had a priority of six centuries over Christianity, so it will not be difficult to say which is the original."

Here are a few, out of many, similarities that the same writer gives about the lives of Jesus and Buddha:

"Both are claimed to have a virgin mother; both had a band of disciples; both taught orally and their teachings were written by others; both lived a life of celibacy; both systems have monasteries; both have images of Virgin and child; both believe in a devil and evil spirits; both believe in casting out devils; both believe in holy water; both use censor with fire chains; both have the doctrine of reincarnation; both teach miracles; both insist that their own system is the most divine and perfect. Buddha taught the commandments as follows:

"Thou shalt not kill; thou shalt not steal; thou shalt not commit adultery: thou shalt not speak untruth; thou shalt not take any intoxicating drink; thou shalt avoid all anger, hatred and bitter language; thou shalt not indulge in idle and vain talk; thou shalt not covet thy neighbor's goods; thou shalt not harbor envy, nor malice, nor the desire of thy neighbor's death or misfortune; thou shalt not follow the doctrines of false gods."

In the time of ancient paganism the most important individual in a community was, generally, believed to have a god for a father—Christna had a virgin mother; Prometheus was half man and half god; Esculapius had the same divine origin. Alexander the Great, aspired to this line of destruction to be on equal terms with the gods. About five hundred years B. C., there was established a law to stop so divine a nuisance! At this progressive era no one with the least intelligence would believe a Messiah that pretended to be a descendant from the gods.

Here is a clipping from the Boston "Investigator," which is further proof where Christianity derived its source in respect to its superstitions:

CHRISTMAS.

"The Christian Church claims that Jesus was born on December 25th. As it does not know on what day he was born, why was this day chosen for his birth-day? Let us see. We find that nearly all the ancient nations on the twenty-fifth of December celebrated the birth of a god. In India the custom of observing Christmas is of great antiquity. The people cover their houses with leaves and flowers, and distribute gifts among their friends.

In China, the time of the winter solstice, the last week of December is celebrated with religious solemnities and business of all kinds is stopped. The same may be said of Persia and Egypt. Buddha is said to have been born on December 25th, so was the Persian Savior Mithras.

The 25th of December was also the birth-day of the Egyptian gods. Hercules, a Greek deity, was born on this same day. Bacchus and Adonis, two more Grecian gods, first saw the light of day on Christmas morn. The Romans also regarded the 25th of December as a holy time, and celebrated the birth of Sol on this day.

Mr. Gibbon, in his "Decline and Fall of the Roman Empire," says: "The Roman Christians, ignorant of the real date of, his (Christ's) birth, fixed the solemn festival to the 25th of December, the Brumalia, or Winter Solstice, when the Pagans annually celebrated the birth of Sol."

We see that Christmas, then, is an ancient and a heathen celebration, and that the Christians adopted the day as the birthday of their god, in order, as they said, "to draw the heathens to the religion of Christ."

The real significance of Christmas is the birth of the sun, the increase of light, the coming of a new year; and this fact was hailed with gladness, and celebrated with games and religious rites, centuries before the birth of Christianity.

Christmas is one of many Pagan festivals to which Christianity adjusted its faith.

There is a wider and deeper meaning to the feelings which are manifested upon this day than any religion can express. Thousands will strive to make human hearts glad who care nothing for the person called Christ. The desire to give happiness to others, that reigns triumphant at this time, does not have birth in any religious emotion. It is impossible to associate even a thought of Christ with the Christmas tide of joy. Christmas has burst its Pagan and Christian importance, and has become the great festival of the human heart. Its character is less and less religious every year and more and more social. It is a day when every one can rejoice to see the darkness leaving, the light coming."

CHRISTMAS AND THE JEWS.

[From the New York Journal.]

According to Rabbi Sonneschein of St. Louis, the American Jew can keep Christmas without in the least violating his religious convictions. The Rabbi says that December 25th, was celebrated by the pagan world as the time when the longest night gives way to the lengthening of the day and that the early Christian Church, which had originally celebrated the natal day of its founder in the spring, accepted at the end of the fifth century the pagan festival, transferring its celebration of Christ's birth to December. Moreover, the Maccabean priests instituted a festival on the 25th, of Kisler, the corresponding Jewish month, to take the place of this pagan feast, when they had by defeating the Syrian King driven out Greek idolatry.

ROMAN CATHOLIC PURGATORY.

[From the Boston Investigator.]

MR. EDITOR: It seems that theoretical purgatory began to be spoken of from the Pagans and Jews in the 6th century, but did not obtain a fixed residence till in the Council of Florence it became an integral part of infallibility, A. D. 1430. Now to more fully understand this "purgatory" business, I thought it most proper to have it described by one who has been through the Roman Catholic Mill, and knows all about it. Anthony Gavin, an ex-priest of Saragossa, in Spain, says:

"I cannot give a real account of purgatory, but I will tell all I know of the practices and doctrines of the Romish priests and friars in relation to that imaginary place, which indeed must be of vast extent and almost infinite capacity, if, as the priests give out, there are as many apartments in it as conditions and ranks of people in the world among Roman Catholics.

"The intenseness of the fire in purgatory is calculated by them, which they assert is eight degrees, and that of hell only four degrees. But there is a great difference between these two fires, in this, viz.: that of purgatory, (though more intense, active, consuming, and devouring,) is but a time, of which the souls may be freed by the suffrages of the masses; but that of hell is forever. In both places, they say, the souls are tormented and deprived of the glorious sight of God; but the souls in purgatory (though they endure a great deal more than those in hell) have certain hopes of seeing God sometime or other, and that hope is enough to make them to be called the blessed souls.

"Pope Adrian the Third, confessed that there was no mention of purgatory in Scripture, or in the writings of the holy fathers; but notwithstanding this, the 'Council of Trent' has settled the doctrine of purgatory without alleging any one passage of Scripture, and gave so much liberty to priests and friars by it, that they build in that fiery palace, apartments for kings, princes, noblemen, grandees, merchants and tradesmen, for ladies of quality, and for gentlewomen and tradesmen's wives, and for poor, common people.

"These are the eight apartments which answer to the eight degrees of intensus ignis, i. e., intense fire; and they make the people believe that the poor people only endure the least degree; the second being greater, is for gentlewomen and tradesmen's wives, and so on to the eighth degree, which being the greatest of all is reserved for kings. By this wicked doctrine they get gradually masses from all sorts of people, in proportion to their greatness. But as the poor cannot give so many masses as the great, the lowest chamber of purgatory is always crowded with the reduced souls of those unfortunately fortunate people, for they say to them that the providence of God has ordered everything to the ease of his creatures, and that foreseeing that the poor people could not afford the same number of masses that the rich could, his infinite goodness had placed them in a place of less suffering in purgatory.

"But it is a remarkable thing that many poor, silly tradesmen's wives, desirous of honor in the next world, ask the friars whether the souls of their fathers, mothers, or sisters, can be removed from the second apartment (reckoning from the lowest) to the third? thinking by it, that although the third degree of fire is greater than the second, yet the soul would be better pleased in the company of ladies of quality; but the worst is, that the friar makes such women believe that he may do it very easily if they give the same price for a mass the ladies of quality give. I knew a shoemaker's wife, very ignorant, proud, and full of punctilios of honor, who went to a Franciscan friar, and told him that she desired to know whether her own father's soul was in purgatory or not, and in what apartment. The friar asked her how many masses she could spare for it? She answered two; and the friar answered, 'Your father's soul is among the beggars.' Upon hearing this, the poor woman began to cry, and desired the friar to put him, if possible, in the fourth apartment, and she would pay him for it; and the quantum being settled, the friar promised to place him there the next day. So the poor woman ever since gives out that her father was a rich merchant, for it was revealed to her that his soul is among the merchants in purgatory!

"Now what can we say but the Pope is the chief Governor of that place, and priests and friars the quartermasters that billet the souls according to their own fancies, and have the power, and give for money, the King's apartments to the soul of a shoemaker, and that of a lady of quality to her washer-woman!

"But mind, reader, how chaste the friars are in procuring a separate place for ladies in purgatory; they suit this doctrine to the temper of a people whom they believe to be extremely jealous, and really not without ground of them, and so no soul of a woman can be placed among men. Many serious people are well pleased with this Christian caution; but those that are given to pleasure do not like it at all, and I knew a pleasant young collegian who went to a friar and said to him—'Father, I own that I love the fair sex, and believe my soul will always retain that inclination.'

"'I am told that no man's soul can be in company with ladies, and it is a dismal thing for me to think that I must go there, (but as for hell I am in no danger of it, thanks to the Pope,) where I never shall see any more women, which will prove the greatest of torments to my soul; so I have resolved to agree with your Reverence beforehand upon this point: I have a bill of ten pistoles upon Peter la Vinna Banquer, and if you can assure me, either to send me straight to heaven when I die, or to the ladies' apartment in purgatory, you shall have the bill; and if you cannot, I must submit to the will of God like a good Christian.'

"The friar seeing the bill, which he supposed was ready money, told him that he could do either of the two, and that he himself might choose which of the two places he pleased. 'But Father,' said the collegian, 'the case is, that I love Donna Teresa Spinola, but she does not love me, and I do not believe that I can expect any favor from her in this world, so I would know whether she is to go before me to purgatory or not.' 'Oh! that is very certain,' said the friar. 'I choose, then,' said the collegian, 'the ladies' apartment, and here is the bill,' &c.

"Now, having given a description of the workings of the Roman Catholic purgatory, and the doings of misguided priest and friar scamps, backed up by Popes and Councils, I will conclude by saying: There is not one text of Scripture to be found in the bible that teaches the Romish dogma of purgatory! So you see their whole system is a scheme to rob the ignorant of their money, to aggrandize Popes and priests? Let the poor dupes read the bible for themselves, and they can soon find out the fraud of Popery.   Yours,

Boston, Oct. 13, 1884.   A. LUTHERITE.

THE BUDDHIST HELL.

Frederic J. Masters, D. D., in the "Californian," March, 1893, writes that:

"Buddhism was introduced into China by Indian missionaries in the first century of the Christian era."

The few extracts declare that:

"Buddhism taught six states of being: gods, men, demons, animals, hungry ghosts and torment in hell. Life is represented as a great wheel, with six spokes, ever turning—an incessant change from one state of being into another—and to be lifted off this transmigration treadmill into the Nirvana of non-being is the strange prospect held out by Gautama Buddha. Until that goal is reached there is no rest, but an incessant ebb and flow of the tides of life, birth and rebirth into states determined by a man's store of accumulated merit or demerit, either in ascending shapes from man up to Buddhahood, or in descending forms of life from man down to worms and slugs.

"Whatever may have been the teachings of the earlier Buddhists on the question of a future life, the popular conception of future retribution entertained by the Chinese, to-day, bears many points of resemblance to that of the Grecian and Roman classics.

"Dante writes over the gates of Hades, 'Abandon hope all ye who enter here.' The Buddhist system is purgatorial and remedial, possessing ten kingdoms, each containing sixteen sub-hells. In the tenth kingdom, in this region, all torment is brought to an end. The punishments endured in successive stages of purgatory are not eternal but temporary and remedial; designed only to wash out all those stains of long-contracted filth that remain in the soul, to cure it of base animal cravings and love of life, so that at last; after long kalpas of time, Buddha's rest of peace is reached.

"In this tenth region is found the mill of transmigration, the wheel of change that turns incessantly ; and ever against the five quagmires of the world are the bridges of fate, built of gold, silver, jade and wood, across which the souls emancipated from purgatory pass to be reborn into the world whether as man, beast, bird, reptile, fish or insect. Upon those who spent their days on earth reading the Sutras, these hells have no power ; their names are in the 'Book of Life' ; a higher sphere on earth awaits them, and their detention in purgatory is very brief. Before their rebirth it is said, these souls are taken by the angel Mang to the Kii Mong pagoda, and made to drink of the broth of oblivion. But whatever joys await the soul in its loftier transportations, this life is not its goal. Buddhism taught that human life is, at its best, a delusion, a curse and a bitterness. Till disenchantment came and a desire was quenched, there was no hope of salvation. Life's chains and trammels must one by one be broken off. The soul must be weaned from ephemeral joys and evanescent pleasures. And to escape this dizzy whirl of life's ever changing wheel, to find release from purgatorial hells, and from the dreary monotony of successive births and deaths, Buddhism showed but one way. It was to renounce the world, take refuge in 'the three precious ones'—Buddha, the Law and the Church, to spend one's life in wrapt meditation and dreary abstraction. So shall blessed tranquility come, the world and all unreal things shall fade away and then comes the end. Just as 'the dewdrop slips into the shining sea,' so life and being, personality and consciousness shall be absorbed in Buddha and swallowed up in Nirvana.

"The great mass of men who could only be restrained from vice by vivid pictures of its future penalties and who could only be made virtuous by promises of eternal reward, found the needed motives in that modified, and more popular form of Buddhism that pictured the bliss of the Western Paradise and the torments of the 160 hells ; and which taught that every act of worship, kind deed, good desire, and holy purpose are unerringly placed to their credit in the ledger of the gods. Confucius over-estimated the national character when he expected a Chinamen to do good without pay, or to be deterred from evil because it was wrong."

The priesthood invented the 160 Buddhistic hells in order to restrain mankind from evil. The key to this mystery is found, and the Christians adopted the pagan myth to benefit a higher civilization by a gigantic pre-varication.

What amount of suffering the Buddhist endures to be annihilated at last ! This belief, however, is preferable to the one that the major portion of humanity is boiling forever in some Stygian Lake.

It is self-evident that in an age of ignorance of the masses, hell and purgatory was invented to restrain the brutal nature by way of fear. It, also, is an easy way to secure money for the benefit of the Lord which makes the contiuance of this belief extremely desirable. Hell and purgatory is a legacy from paganism ! Whenever more money is needed for the Lord the beauty and grandeur of the satanic kingdom is portrayed with eloquence and the laity pay more money cheerfully to please the Great Jehovah !

A man asked a deacon this question:

"What do you propothe to do with the money?" "Give it to the Lord," replied the deacon. "Well, thir said the man, "ath I think my chantheth of theeing the Lord are ath good ath yours, I prefer to wait and hand it to him in perthon," and he put his half dollar in his pocket.

How many honestly think what would teachers of men talk about, if they could not explain the mysteries of salvation year after year.

Let the churches echo the voice of science. It is a field as broad as the universe and as grand as immensity.

This little planet, though but an atom in comparison with the infinity of worlds, is a ball of grandeur that is a book whose every page is aglow with light and beauty.

The science of life is hardly understood and it would yield a great benefit to mankind to know how to live properly in this world.

Reforms in all classes of society are required to give civilization an impetus in the right direction. The Catholic priests say:

"If a Catholic did wander away from Catholocism he would die a Catholic."

Bruno would not kiss the cross when tied to a stake. It is a libel on the intelligent Catholic. If the priesthood would tell the truth, always, they would command more respect from the masses. It is found Thomas Paine and Voltaire are not atheists, but both believed in one God of Mercy—Voltaire had a chapel erected on his farm at Ferney.

When Jesus was suffering excruciating pain upon the cross, did he vilify his enemies? Did he curse them? Did he excommunicate them?

Admit the existence of a hell, God is responsible for the fiery prison. If he could not control one of his angels in heaven, he is a very weak school-master. If he allowed him to prey upon weak humanity then he and Satan are partners in crime.

If God and Satan could rejoice in the miseries of mankind then God is on the level, in injustice, with the devil. Isaiah says God created evil. In another place,

God laughs at the calamities of his people. It seems as though the bible places the great Jehovah on the same plane with barbarians. Moses and the priesthood could not picture their God any higher, morally, than themselves.

The priesthood like to inspire awe in the minds of their followers. They being representatives of God and Jesus, they wish to be regarded as exceedingly holy. The saints that are worshiped are intended to encourage the devotees to become reverential A picture of a saint with a long face and eyes looking upward is an example for earthly saints when they are in church— and on the Sabbath day.

At one time in the history of the world lived what was termed pillar saints. Simon Stylites resided 37 years on the top of a column, part of that time the column was 40 cubits high.

There was one redeeming quality about the pillar saints, they did persecute their fellow men.

If Jesus had happened to pass by one of these saints, he would have denounced his hypocracy, and bade him have less conceit and to come down from the column and study awhile in the school of common sense, and by living justly leave a lasting influence for the good of humanity. Jesus did not waste any time in meditation on some lofty mountain, neither did he resort to the seclusion of a cloister and study the old superstitions, but inscribed his name on the heart of humanity, which will never fade in its inherent light of divinity. He did not give an esthetic, mental scream whenever crime was mentioned and thought he was too near God to soil his mind with dealing with the reforms of his day. He instituted no harsh measure that leagues were necessary to protect mankind from his influence. No, Jesus was imbued with kindness, love, and goodwill toward men, women and children.

SERMON IN THE SYNAGOGUE.

Jesus, clothed in costly raiment and dazzling jewels, preaches to his congregation thus:

"Verily, I say unto you, that while you live upon earth be as conservative as possible.

"The poor should be ignored, for they are not cultured, and their influence degrading to those used to the refinement of good clothes. Reduce their wages often, for they are not as sensitive, as a class, as you are.

"Be sure and enact laws to fine and imprison persons that heal the sick by the laying on of hands.

"Do not fail to pray in public, and be sure to ask a large salary to reward you for your trouble."

A little child wandered, aimlessly, near where he stood and he took it in his arms. Said he:

"This child is full of 'original sin' and is totally depraved. Unless it is baptized in holy salt and water it will burn forever in endless torment!"

The mother screamed and went out of the Synagogue never more to believe in such pious teachings. Jesus resumed his remarks by saying that:

"Mothers had no rights that the priesthood should respect in regard to making amendments to the Church laws, for 'infant damnation' is an exceedingly humane text to preach to believers as one of my doctrines!

"The men in this congregation should seclude themselves and continually contemplate the Deity. God would be benefited thereby, and so would humanity! Be sure and view Eve's daughters as a near relative to satan and remember she brought sin into the world and it is your duty to keep her under strict surveillance, lest she has any happiness when she is in your company !

"It is wise to invent rituals to quarrel about, for by so doing you keep yourselves unspotted from the world.

"Do not descend to the lower levels of humanity unless you can secure their gold to your glory and honor. Keep within the Church ring, socially, and do not argue with an unbeliever, for our religion will not bear investigation ! Persecute your neighbors with as much ardor as you love yourselves !

"I portend that Titus, the Roman general, will surround Jerusalem, and John and Simon within the gates. Jewish generals, fighting each other and Jerusalem falls an easy prey to the Romans. I see, also, Christians will have various generals within their respective armies, or different denominations expire on the moral plane by the vindictive attitude they possess for each other. Infidelity like the Romans will conquer, and humanity rise in its majesty unshackled by the chains of superstition.

At that moment Jesus saw his chariot, drawn by four horses, coming toward the synagogue, and he dismissed his congregation by saying: "You must be thankful to my two fathers in heaven, which were the same as myself, all being each other's fathers and yet, only one, for the blessings you enjoy. Amen."

CHAPTER V.

Bible Errors.

According to Kersey Graves' "Bible of Bibles" the bible contains two hundred and seventy-seven contradictions. He writes on page 134:

"It is difficult to conceive how any real benefit or any reliable instruction can be derived from a book which contains statements with respect to doctrines or matters of fact that are contradicted on the next page, or in some other portion of the book ; because it not only confuses the mind of the reader, but renders it impossible for him to know, as he reads a statement in one chapter of the book, that it is not contradicted and nullified in some other chapter, until he has sacrificed sufficient time to commit the whole book to memory, and but few persons have ever achieved that herculean task. Hence it must be an unreliable book as authority."

The following are some of the contradictions, copied from "Bible of Bibles" showing the infallibility of the supposed divine word.

"Is God omnipotent? Yes. ' With God all things are possible.' (Matt. xix :26). No. 'He could not drive out the inhabitants of the valley, because their chariots were made of iron.' (Judges, i :19).

"Is God unchangeable? Yes. 'I change not.' (Mal. iii :6). No. 'And God repented of the evil that he had said that he would do unto them.' (Jno. iii :10).

"Has any man seen God? Yes. 'Moses, Aaron, Nadab, and Abihu, and the seventy elders of Israel saw the God of Israel,' etc. (Exod. xxiv :9). No. ' No man hath seen God at any time.' (John i :18). Yes. 'I have seen God face to face, and my life has been preserved.' (Gen. xxxii :30). No. 'There shall no man see me, and live.' (Exod. xxxiii :20). Yes. 'I saw, also, the Lord sitting upon a throne.' (Isa. vi :1). No. 'Ye have neither heard his voice at any time, nor seen his shape.' (John v :37).

"Is it right to kill? No. 'Thou shalt not kill.' Yes. 'Thus saith the Lord God of Israel. Put every man his sword by his side, and go in and out from gate to gate throughout the camp, and slay every man his brother, and every man his companion, and every man his neighbor.' (Exod. xxxii :27).

"Who can know whether the goldenrule is right or

wrong? Right. 'Whatsoever ye would that men should do unto you, do ye even so to them.' (Matt. vii :12). Wrong. 'Spare them not, but slay both man and woman and infant.' (Sam. xv :3).

"At what hour was Christ crucified? Mark says (xv :25), 'It was the third hour.' But according to John, (xix :14), 'It was about the sixth hour.'

"How was Christ dressed for the crucifixion? 'Put on him a scarlet robe.' (Math. xxvii :28). 'They put on him a purple robe.' (John xix :2).

"What was the drink offered to Christ at the crucifixion? Mark says it was wine mixed with myrrh but he received it not. (xv :23).

"Matthew says it was vinegar and Luke also represents it as being vinegar. (xxiii :36). According to John's statement: 'Now there was set a vessel full of vinegar, and they filled a sponge with vinegar, and put it upon hyssop, and put it to his mouth. When Jesus, therefore, had received the vinegar, he said: 'It is finished,' etc., (xix :29,30).

"Who bore Christ's cross? Matthew says, 'And as they came out, they found a man of Cyrene, Simon by name; him they compelled to bear the cross.' (xxvii :32). But John says Jesus bore it himself. (xix :27). 'Thou shalt not bow down thyself unto them, nor serve them: for I, the Lord thy God, am a jealous God,' etc."

The Christians serve three gods and a goddess.

"Honor thy father and thy mother, as the Lord thy God hath commanded thee," etc.

Jesus changed his ideas when he said:

"If any man come to me, and hate not his father and mother, and wife and children, and brethren, and sisters, yea, and his own life, also, he cannot be my disciple." (Luke xiv :26).

Jesus taught the golden rule and he never could be guilty of using such language. It was, no doubt, the work of designing priests, who cared nothing for the happiness of home life. This verse gave their devotees a power to persecute an unbeliever, which has embittered members in families to an extent beyond all human calculations.

Church society cannot frown on the event if one of its lady members separate from her family and unites with a community of a supposed Messiah. Their bible teaches, to hate is a desirable attribute in matters of belief, so it seems to be another phase of bible morality.

If a Catholic priest wishes to leave his surplice, for the purpose of becoming a married man, consequently, a respectable member in society, can, if he wishes, leave wife and children and return to the priesthood with impunity! To hate wife and children is not immoral in the Church, but how very improper for worldly people to separate, for good reasons that are sanctioned by a lofty sense of justice.

In writing about the errors of the bible it does not signify that aught it contains that is beautiful, in fact and sentiment, is not appreciated, perhaps, far more than many who believe the book is a holy production.

Whoever wrote the bible about Moses, wrote a bold hand, making his character the most remarkable of any on record. It is evident that he intended to convey the idea that Moses was equal with God in his manifestations or miracles. He is the one meant, no doubt, when the chronicler says: "God is a man of war!" Another statement, "And the Lord said unto Moses: See, I have made thee a god to Pharaoh, and Aaron, thy brother, shall be thy prophet."

God was certainly inferior to Moses when Moses had the power and inclination to counsel him and to soothe his temper   Their temper was somewhat of equal force, showing that a leader or priest builds the character of his god no higher than himself, morally!   A man that committed murder, as Moses killed the Egyptian, in true bandit style, was just the man to write upon the tablets "thou shalt not kill" and then before the glory of the divinity had disappeared from his face get exceedingly angry, and massacre three thousand of his own people for a little difference of opinion.

"Thou shalt not steal," appeared upon the tablet. After the Israelites borrowed jewelry from the Egyptians it seemed no disgrace to murder the nations with whom they came in contact and then to appropriate unto themselves their goods, which agrees with the beautiful words upon the tablet—"thou shalt not steal." The Jews must have borrowed considerable valuables from the Egyptians for they were far from being poor, by many indications, on their journey toward the land flowing with milk and honey. Moses made his people believe that they should be killed if they ventured to climb Mt. Sinai, where he and God were in social converse.   He was making proper conditions for his communion with God and did not want any one to discover the illuminated paraphernalia, etc.   Moses was learned in the wisdom of the Egyptians, and was a magician, also.

The first account given of Mt. Sinai, stone tablets are not mentioned. The second records the appearance of the tablets but they are not broken by the anger of Moses. The story increases with age, and a graphic description appears in the third record the stones are broken, and his high-handed career commences as a murderer worthy of the one that committed the crime of killing an Egyptian, as Moses did, and then hiding him in the sand! The fourth revelation states that Moses received two more tables of stone, with the law, etc., inscribed upon them. The question arises, where are those tablets? The angels took the Mormon's written messages upon golden stones to heaven, after translation into a book, or Mormon bible. That is a fine way to preserve them—from contact with mortal vision! There is no doubt, but that such a man existed as Moses, and he knew how to write, went up Mt. Sinai and selected some stones and inscribed the ten commandments and the laws, many that were borrowed from Egyptian statutes.

St. Luke, chapter ninth, gives an account of Moses and Elias appearing to Jesus. Jesus wished to go up on a mountain to pray, and he had John and James and Peter go with him. It must have surprised them all to meet with angels, who left such a pure record while on earth. Jesus had so much respect for the laws of Moses, it was quite natural that Moses would come to him!

Again, it does not agree with the Seventh Day Adventist's belief. They, Moses and Elias, should have stayed in their graves until Gabriel blew his trumpet at the last day of the world's history.

The monstrous hallucination about the second coming of Christ will never leave the minds of the deluded until they read the words of the prophecy themselves and judge the meaning by common sense.

When many break away from the thralldom of the creeds, go to the opposite extreme and dèny a belief in any thing appertaining to the divine, in process of time, many of that class, by using reason, take a medium course, become less positive and more susceptible to truth.

Again, there is another kind of mentality that never thinks on any subject, who come out of the Churches and believe something that is as unreasonable as the creeds. Reason's wings are very small at first, but by exercise théy grow to grand proportions and soar in the ether cf cultivated imagination, proudly as the eagle, who basks in the sunlight of his mountain home, or eyrie on some gigantic cliff upon the sea shore.

CHAPTER VI.

Church and State.

A few years ago an able speech was delivered in Congress by Senator Reagan of Texas. He said:

"The history of the world is full of the dangers of the Church and State, and the framers of our government desired to protect this nation from any such danger.

"We find that for several years considerable appropriations have been made for the education of the Indians in contract schools. In one year fifteen denominations received $204,993 while thé Catholics were allowed $359,967 !"

Appropriations for various Catholic institutions have been given in New York City which amount to vast sums of public money and used for sectarian purposes.

No wonder Senator Reagan exclaims that:

'It is an unnatural condition of things in this country—one that ought to be frowned down, and voted down, and put out of existence."

If all the States would act as promptly as Nevada in resisting the demands of the Catholics, there would be no trouble in this respect. When the Sisters of Charity wished an appropriation of the people's money for the benefit of their Orphan Asylum in Virginia City, the bill was defeated before it became a law. The people's money represent the taxes paid by all classes and it is decidedly wrong. It is in the same category of morals, as breaking into a neighbor's house when all the inmates are unconscious, and appropriating that which does not belong to the burglar.

The taxes paid to the Government is supposed to be in the keeping of honest officials to pay expenses and to use it for the benefit of all wherever it is needed—not to be given to a few who despise the State and would return the favor by crushing out the liberties of those from whom they took money that did not belong to them.

THE SCHOOL AMENDMENT.

In Congress, the Senator from Massachusetts (Mr. Hoar) presented recently a petition signed by 3,228 citizens of Massachusetts, praying for the adoption of a constitutional amendment which will prohibit the interference of any religious sect with the system of common public schools. The petition is as follows:

"*To the Honorable Senate and Members of the House of Representatives in Washington, D. C. :*

"We, the undersigned citizens of Massachusetts, sensibly impressed with the importance of education among the people of our land, in the conservation of our Government and the liberties which we so richly enjoy ;

believing, also, as expressed in a late public gathering of patriotic citizens of Boston, in old Faneuil Hall, 'it has now become necessary to guard well the public school as the palladium of our liberty;' and being persuaded also that this desired protection will be more fully affected by a provision in the fundamental laws of the land (as urged upon Congress by that eminent and patriotic citizen, General Grant, while in the Presidential office,) would respectfully petition your honorable bodies to speedily frame such article for submission to the Legislatures of the several States, for their approval or rejection, as will prevent the interference of any religious sect with the 'common school system' or the appropriating of any of the 'public funds' for sectarian uses; such a measure as this being, in our judgment, the only safeguard against religious encroachments, such as now threaten our time-honored, and truly endeared methods of teaching and training our youth for the duties and responsibilities of American citizenship; to the end, also, that there may be preserved to us and transmitted to our children's children 'a government of the people, by the people, and for the people.'"

ITALY'S FREE SCHOOLS, 1891.

"The Italian government has commenced at the right end in its efforts to inculcate patriotism in the hearts of the rising generation. It has taken possession of the schools, and young Italy is being taught that its first allegiance is to king and country, instead of to Pope and Church. A system of compulsory free education has been established, and no school is allowed to remain open which does not comply with the government requirements. Many of the Italian children, however, are being educated in parish schools, but these institutions are not permitted to run upon the free-and-easy, go-as-you-please system which characterizes the parochial schools in the United States. The government insists that in every parish school the text-books used shall be those authorized by the government; that all the teachers must be those authorized by the government; that all scholars must pass an examination by the government inspectors, and that the portrait of the king must be in every school-room.

"This system of national education has brought about a wondrous change. In 1870 the percentage of illiteracy in Rome was 90 per cent.; now it is barely 45. The children are growing up thoroughly patriotic and loyal to the government. The Pope cuts every day less and less of a political factor in Italian affairs. Education and civil and religious liberty are driving out ignorance and priestly tyranny. The school house is proving more than a match for the vatican."

"In liberty loving America the Jesuits voted down the Constitution under which New Mexico Territory was to enter Statehood, their objection being in its provision of public, in place of their parochial schools. This keeps New Mexico out of the Union at present."

Nov. 12th, 1890.   —*Exchange.*

In proportion as civilization advances to a higher standard of perfection, revolutions are regulated without bloodshed, as in the case of the Mormons being made to pass on to a more humane life and leave the superstition as a grave on the highway of life. Another instance is recorded of Mexico; although a Catholic country, it was disgusted with the followers of Jesus—the Jesuits. The following extracts were printed in 1876. They are:

"Twenty years ago, two-thirds of the real estate in Mexico was owned by the Romish Church, but, as the result of the mighty uprising of the past fifteen years against the Church oligarchy, Mexico has now not a monk, nun, Sister of Charity or Jesuit within its borders. Bishop Butler tells thrilling stories of the Inquisition in Mexico, which has been overthrown within twenty years. The old Inquisition buildings at Pueblo are now owned by the Methodist mission, and Dr. Butler has with his own hands removed skeletons of men and woman from the cells in which, he says, not many years ago they were walled in and left to die, like Marmions Constance at Holy Isle. The headquarters of the mission in the city of Mexico, are in the former palace of the last Montezuma, which had, for more than 300 years been used as a Franciscan convent till the confiscation of Church property by the General Government."

When the yoke was broken between Church and State, how quickly universal toleration was proclaimed. The account reads:

"The press was made free; free schools established and universal toleration. The whole Church property became the property of the State—the clergy only tenants by courtesy. No such a bold and radical change was ever before made in a Catholic country."

The Independent, Henderson Co., Minn., paper has this advice:

"A young lady residing in St. Paul, the only daughter of a Protestant mother, was sent to St. Joseph's Academy to secure an education. She graduated and returned home, but shortly after ran away and entered a convent. The mother was nearly broken hearted at the affair, but this had no effect on the girl, as the sisters had told her that it was her duty to renounce the world and enter a convent, EVEN IF IT KILLED HER MOTHER. Parents should take warning by this. If you care anything for the love of your children, let them get an education in public schools, and let all religious institutions severely alone."

THE "BLACK VEIL."

The eccentric doings of "Father" Ignatius, an ultra Ritualist of the English Church, have made him notorious for many years. The London "Truth" thus describes one of his latest official acts:

" An extraordinary scene was witnessed at Llanthony Abbey on Sunday week, when Father Ignatius admitted a novice to the mysteries of the "Black Veil." Opposite the principle shrine was a black funeral bier, covered with a velvet pall, with white cross and a huge candle stick at each corner. The novice knelt by its side. After mass and a sermon, the "Father Abbot" sat down in his chair by the altar, arrayed in a gorgeous robe, embroidered with angels and saints, with a rich jeweled mitre on his shaven head, and a crosier in his hand. The nuns in their grated gallery sang a chant, while the father cut off the hair of the novice, two acolytes holding a towel to receive it. Then she was clad in her nun's robes, with a crimson veil and a wreath of flowers, and, after a variety of intricate ceremonies, she was placed on a throne-like chair before the altar, and the whole of the monks, sisters and acolytes prostrated themselves before her, and as they kissed the hem of her garment she placed her hands on their heads. After the procession she was laid on the bier and covered with a pall, and the abbot and acolytes came forward in a magpie like costume of black and white, the "father" with a high, caul cap-like linen-mitre on his head. Then the funeral service was chanted, a muffled bell sounded, and the monks bore away bier and nun behind the gratings.

This nation should never allow a nunnery on its soil, for it is a kingdom where the priest rules with despotic power over the life and liberty of young ladies. It is contrary to the spirit of justice and humanity.

CATHOLICISM.

[The Boston Investigator.]

MR. EDITOR :—Father Chiniquy, who is preaching around here, is an ex-Catholic, now 80 years old, and for 25 years was a Romish priest. He says, in one of his reported sermons :

" The Roman Catholic Church is blasphemous and idolatrous. Its members were honest, but the priests practised deception, and inculcated horrible and diabolical ideas into the minds of their parishioners to make them confess their sins. The priests were thieves when they pretended that they could take souls out of purgatory by accepting large sums of money from relatives of dead people. The Roman Catholic Church was not founded by Christ or the apostles. There was not a word of God in it. Its principal idea was to make . money and preach the false traditions of men instead of the gospel in the bible.

" He described in a feeling manner his conversion from Romanism to Protestantism. He told of his missionary work as a Catholic priest in Canada and the Western States and said that now he might have been one of the heads of the Roman Catholic hierarchy in the United States, if he had not accepted the Protestant religion. The Pope had offered him the highest honors for his services, and the Canadian Parliament had presented him with a gold medal, as a compliment to his missionary labors. In closing he called upon every Protestant to awaken to the signs of the times. The Roman Catholics were bound to conquer if they could. Protestants must maintain their rights and resist every encroachment of the Catholics tending toward Church and State. Eternal life was the gift only of the Saviour, and not of a man in priestly garb, who pretended he could blot out sins in the confessional."

THE JESUITS.

This order of the Roman Catholic Church, was instituted in 1535, and became so notorious for its lax system of morals, ambition, and intrigues, that sentence of abolition against it was passed by the Government of almost every civilized nation; and, at last, in 1773, by Pope Clement XIV, (who was poisoned by them the year after.) A bull was issued for the restoration of the order of the Jesuits in 1814, by Pope Pius VII.

Since that time the Jesuits have continued their work all over the world. There are a great many of them in this country—in fact, the United States are their strong hold, as they have been driven out of nearly all Europe. They are a dangerous set, and need watching. In Italy, as may be seen by the following, the Government is very severe with them, far more so than our own Government:

Italy has banished from all her educational institutions the Jesuit and the priest, not as a high official of the Government recently said, "because the Government is opposed to religion, but because she fears the traitor." The Jesuit and the priest have constantly been intriguing against popular government in Austria, Italy, and France. In Italy the Jesuits and priests in great numbers were taken as spies of their enemies, they were even allies of the brigan s, and are intensely in favor of the temporal power of the Pope.

The Italian Government will not allow this insidious work, and thus at present is carefully watching, and is expelling from the school-rooms secret priests, who have insinuated suggestions of the recovery of temporal power, since the Papal jubilee, and since the Ultramontane party has become bolder. The Government is dealing severely with these traitors, who are trying to establish a foreign power in the State, and in the schools. It banishes from the schools all teachers in favor of the reinstatement of the Papal rule.—[Transcript.

There is a conflict between many of our public schools and the Catholics. It is wise to watch the various schemes adopted to carry out their programme; to watch also the operations of the Clan-na-Gael, a secret society which carries out the orders for the Chief who resides at Rome.

A. J. Grover states that:

"It is well known that Mr. Blaine sought and expected the Jesuits' support; it is well known that the Clan-na-Gael supported him; that Pat Egan, Alexander Sullivan and all the leaders of that secret conclave of conspirators were his friends and he theirs. They believed the Republican party would continue in power and Alexander Sullivan would have a cabinet office under Blaine. No doubt Blaine had promised to appoint him, deep-dyed with the blood of Hanford as he was, Jesuit as he is, embezzler as he is."

Again, he says:

"It is proven that the funds of the Clan-na-Gael were not used for the cause of Ireland. It was a pretence, to cover the real purpose, which was to destroy the public schools and run the politics of the country. Alexander Sullivan began by killing a school-master of leading influence who was opposed to Roman Catholic control of the Chicago schools. The Jesuits saved their leader and tool from the gallows.

"The order of the Society of Jesus has very large control of the press, pulpit, political parties, and almost absolute control of some of the Chicago courts and the police force. When this great secret organization can seize a national party, form an alliance with its leaders and shape its policy, what can be done? When it can with impunity and undiscovered by the public remove Presidents who will not do their bidding, as it did Lincoln, if not Garfield; when it can bring to this country its method and practices in the old world for hundreds of years, by which liberty has been perpetually destroyed, what do the people propose to do? We shall see. The Jesuits killed Hanford; the Jesuits killed Cronin; the Jesuits killed Lincoln. The first, to promote their schemes to control the public schools; the second, to prevent the exposure of their appropriation of Irish funds to their political purposes in this country; and their political purposes are to control national parties and ultimately make this country politically subject to the temporal power of the Pope. Will not honest men and women see that Popery and liberty cannot live in this same country? This country is large, but there is not room for both."

It is well for all persons who are loyal to their country to read the bills and laws that are printed in the papers about the work of the United States Congress, and, also, every State in the Union.

See the modest demand, of the missionaries belonging to the Methodist Episcopal Church, who desired the repeal of the . Geary Chinese Exclusion Law. They petitioned Congress from China for the reason they were afraid the Chinese would destroy their property they valued at $400,000,000. They were very patriotic when they rather have this Republic crushed and destroyed by paganism than to lose the paltry sum of $400,000,000.

THE MURDER OF ABRAHAM LINCOLN.

Planned and Executed by Jesuit Priests.

[The Boston Investigator.]

MR. EDITOR: Ninety miles Northwest of St. Paul, (Minn.,) is the little village of St. Joseph, settled by Roman Catholics, and with a college for the education of priests. On the 14th of April, 1865, at 6 o'clock in the afternoon, two men drove up to the village hotel; one was the Rev. F. A. Conwell, chaplain of the First Minnesota Regiment, the other was Horace P. Bennett, a resident of St. Cloud, about ten miles eastward. While Mr. Bennett was attending to the horses in the barn, the landlord, J. H. Linneman, who had charge of the friary and was a purveyor for the priests, told

chaplain Conwell that President Lincoln and Secretary
Seward were assassinated. And when Mr. Bennett returned from the barn to the tavern, the landlord repeated the statement to both his guests.

This was not later than 6.30 P. M., and the assassination of Lincoln did not occur until about 10 P. M.
Allowing for the difference in time between St. Joseph
and Washington, the news of the assassination had
apparently reached St. Joseph at least two hours before it occurred !

Early the next morning the two men went to St.
Cloud, arriving there about 8 o'clock. There Mr.
Conwell told the hotel keeper, Haworth, what he had
heard about the assassination of Lincoln and Seward.
He told it also to several other men. None of them had
heard such news. The nearest railroad station from St.
Joseph was forty miles, and the nearest telegraph
eighty miles.

The next day, April 16, was Sunday, and Chaplain
Conwell started for Church, where he was to preach.
On his way a copy of a telegram was handed him an-
nouncing the assassination of Lincoln and Seward.

On Monday, April 17, Mr. Conwell addressed the St.
Paul Press the following paragraph :

A STRANGE COINCIDENCE.

"At 6.30 P. M., Friday last, April 14, I was told as
an item of news, eight miles west of this place (St. Cloud,)
that Lincoln and Seward had been assassinated."

This was published, but the fact being discredited by
the editor, another communication was sent by Mr. Conwell which was printed as follows :

"The integrity of history requires that the above coincidence be established. And if any one calls it in
question, than proofs more ample than reared their
sanguinary shadows to comfort the traitor can now be
given."

Was this merely "a strange coincidence ?" Emphatically, no! The priests of St. Joseph knew that Abraham Lincoln and other heads of the national Government were to be assassinated on Friday, April 14, 1865.

The first intimation that came to the ears of Abraham Lincoln that he was to become a victim to the vengeance of the Romish priesthood was as early as October, 1856. Twice in that year he had defended a Catholic priest, Father Chiniquy, of St. Anne, (Illinois,) before a jury, on a false accusation of crime. The first trial was in May, 1856, at Urbana, seventy miles distant˙ from the accused. Mr. Lincoln demolished the testimony of two perjured priests and his client would have been acquitted but for the blunder of allowing a single Roman Catholic on the jury.

The case was tried again in October following. The testimony of a priest, named LeBelle, against the character of Father Chiniquy was of such a nature as to horrify everybody. The cross-examination by Mr. Lincoln did much to break the force of the direct testimony, but he feared its effects upon a jury unacquainted with the character of his client. When the court adjourned in the evening Mr. Lincoln said:

"My dear Mr. Chiniquy, though I hope to-morrow to destroy the testimony of LeBelle, I must concede that I see great danger ahead. I feel that the jurymen think you guilty, and that you will be condemned to a heavy penalty or to the penitentiary, though I am sure you are perfectly innocent. It is very probable that we shall have to confront LeBelle's sister to-morrow, who will confirm the false testimony of her brother. Her alleged sickness is doubtless a feint, in order that her evi lence may come in after that of her brother. And perhaps we shall have to meet her testimony as taken before some local justice, which will be all the harder to rebut. That woman is evidently in the hands of Bishop O'Regan and her brother, ready to swear to anything they order her. Nothing is so difficult to refute as female testimony, particularly when the woman is absent from court. The only way to be sure of a favorable verdict to-morrow is, that God Almighty would take part and show your innocence. Go to him, for he alone can save you."

These words are as recorded by Father Chiniquy himself, and they are perhaps a little colored, coming through the medium of a very pious and conscientious priest, who was to renounce the error of Papacy and become a devout Protestant. Sadly Father Chiniquy betook himself to his room, where, through the night, he wrestled in prayer. It was an awful night of agony. But at 3 o'clock there was loud knocking at his door. Quickly the tearful priest opened it and there stood Abraham Lincoln, who said:

"Cheer up, my dear Chiniquy, I have the perjured priests in my hands. Their diabolical plot is known and if they do not fly away before the dawn of day they will surely be lynched. Bless the Lord, you are saved."

The next morning the court-house could not contain the crowd that came to see the result of that trial. The perjured priest LeBelle had fled, but there were numerous other holy fathers present hoping to witness the condemnation of the French Canadian priest. Judge David Davis took his seat on the bench and the complainant Spink, a tool of Bishop O'Regan, rose, pale and trembling, to ask to be allowed to withdraw the prosecution. The motion was of course granted, but the miserable priests in attendance were then regaled with a most eloquent and scathing speech by Abraham Lincoln on the rascality of this prosecution, and the infamous character of the Romish priesthood in general.

Accepting a fee of only fifty dollars for his services, Lincoln turned to his client and said, "Father Chiniquy, what makes you weep? You ought to be the most happy man alive ; you have beaten your enemies and gained a most glorious victory."

"Dear Mr. Lincoln," answered the priest, "the joy I should naturally feel for such a victory is turned to grief when I think of its consequence to you. Not less than ten or twelve Jesuit priests came from Chicago and St. Louis to hear my sentence of condemnation. But instead of that you have brought the thunders of heaven on their heads ; you have made the walls of the court-house tremble with your denunciation of their infamy. They are enraged, and I fear that I have read your death sentence in their bloody eyes."

At first Lincoln treated the warning lightly, but afterwards said, "I know the Jesuits never forget or forgive ; but what matters it how or where a man dies, provided it is at the post of duty ? "

The election of Lincoln to the presidency was unanimously opposed by the Catholic priests. The Church of Rome looked upon the division between North and South as her golden opportunity in America. She ordered her elder son, the Emperor of France, to send an army to Mexico so as to be ready to help crush the Northern States. She bade the bishops, priests, and people to vote in opposition to Abraham Lincoln. Only one Bishop dared to disobey.

Father Chiniquy had now renounced the Papist creed and become a devout Protestant. At the end of August, 1861, a Roman priest whom he had persuaded to leave the errors of Popery, disclosed to him a plot to assassinate the President. He thought it his duty to go and tell him of it. He was received with great cordiality by Mr. Lincoln, who said :

" You see that your friends, the Jesuits, have not killed me yet. But they would have done it when I went through Baltimore had I not defeated their plans by passing incognito a few hours before they expected me. We have the proof that the company selected and organized to murder me was led by a rabid Roman Catholic named Byrne, and that in the gang were two disguised priests. I am sorry to have so little time to see you, but I will not let you go before telling you that a few days ago Prof. Morse told me that when he was in Rome, not long ago, he found the proofs of a formidable conspiracy against this country and its institutions. It is evident that it is to the intrigues and emissaries of the Pope, that we owe, in a great part, this horrible Civil War."

The next day, Chiniquy was received again by the President. "I want your views," said Lincoln, "about a thing that is exceedingly puzzling to me. A great number of Democratic papers have been sent to me lately, containing statements that I am an apostate Roman Catholic. No priest of Rome ever laid his hand on my head. Tell me what is the meaning of these falsehoods?"

"It means your sentence of death," said Chiniquy, "and I have it from the lips of a converted priest that in order to execute the fanaticism of Roman Catholic murderers, the priests have invented the false story of your being born a Catholic and being baptized by a priest. An apostate from the Church of Rome is an outcast who has no right to live. Here is a copy of a decree of Gregory VII, proclaiming that the killing of an apostate or a heretic is not murder. Such is the canon law of the Catholic Church."

Realizing the imminent danger, Mr. Lincoln said:

"I repeat to you what I said at Urbana in 1856, when you first warned me against the Jesuits. But I will now add that I have a presentiment that God will call me through the hand of an assassin. Let his will be done. I feel more and more that it is not against the South alone we are fighting, but against the Pope of Rome and his perfidious Jesuits, who are the principal rulers of the South. The great majority of the Catholic bishops, priests and laymen, are rebels in heart, and, with few exceptions, they are pro-slavery! I understand now why the patriots of France were compelled to kill so many priests and monks; they were and always are the enemies of Liberty."

Again, in June, 1862, Father Chiniquy called on the President to warn him against impending dangers, but could only shake hands with him. It was just after the grand victory of the Monitor over the Merrimac, and the conquest of New Orleans by Admiral Farragut, and Mr. Lincoln was too busy to grant an interview.

Once more in June, 1864, came Chiniquy to Washington, and the President managed to have an interview with him by taking him in his carriage to visit the wounded soldiers in the hospital. Mr. Lincoln said:

"This war would never had been possible without the sinister influence of the Jesuits. We owe it all to Popery. I conceal this from the knowledge of the nation, because if the people knew what I do, this would become a religious war and assume a tenfold more savage and bloody character. If the people could know what Prof. Morse has told me of the plots at Rome to destroy this Republic, if they could realize that the priests, monks, and nuns who land on our shores under the pretext of propagating their religion, teaching our children, and nursing the sick in our hospitals, are only the emissaries of the Pope and the other despots of Europe, to undermine our institutions and propose a reign of anarchy here as they have done in Ireland, in Mexico, and in Spain, the Protestants, both North and South, would surely unite to exterminate the priests of Rome."

The President then asked Mr. Chiniquy if he had read the letter of the Pope to Jeff Davis; and if so what he thought of it. The ex-priest replied:

"My dear President, that is just what brought me here again. That letter is a poisoned arrow aimed by the Pope at you personally. You know how many liberty-loving Irish, German, and French Catholics have been fighting for the Union. To detach these men from the ranks of the Northern armies has been the aim of the Jesuits. Secret and pressing letters have been addressed from Rome to the bishops, ordering them to weaken your armies by detaching these men. The bishops answered that they could not do it without exposing themselves to death, but they advised the Pope to recognize at once the legitimacy of the Southern Republic, and to take Jeff Davis under his protection by a letter which would be read everywhere. By that letter his blind slaves understand that you are outraging the God of heaven and earth by continuing this bloody war to subdue a nation whose legitimacy is recognized by God's vicegerent. That letter means that you are not only an apostate whom every Catholic has a right to kill, but you are a lawless brigand whom every Catholic ought to kill. This, my dear President, is not a fanciful interpretation of my own ; it is the unanimous explanation given me by a great number of priests at Rome, with whom I have had occasion to speak on this subject. I conjure you, therefore, to protect your precious life.''

The President replied at great length, saying :

"You confirm me in my view of the Pope's letter, and Prof. Morse is of the same mind with you. Since the publication of that letter there have been many desertions. But Gen. Sheridan remains true to his oath of fidelity and is worth a whole army by his ability and courage. Gen. Meade has gained the battle at Gettysburg, but he was surrounded by such heroes as Reynolds, Wadsworth, Slocum, Sickles, Hancock, Howard, and others. And yet he let the rebel army escape. When he was to order the pursuit, a stranger came to him in haste; that stranger was a disguised Jesuit. After ten minutes' conversation with him, Meade made such arrangements for the pursuit that the enemy escaped almost untouched, with the loss of only two guns. The New York draft riots were the work of Bishop Hughes and his emissaries. We have the proofs in hand of that. I wrote to Bishop Hughes, telling him that the whole country would hold him responsible if he did not stop the riots at once. He then gathered the rioters around his palace, called them his dear friends, invited them to go back home peacefully, and they obeyed. The Pope and his Jesuits have aided and supported the rebellion from the first gun-shot at Fort

Sumter by the rabid Roman, Beauregard. They are helping the Roman Catholic Semmes, on the ocean. I have the proof in hand that Bishop Hughes, whom I sent to Rome in the hope that he would induce the Pope to urge American Catholics to be true to their oath of allegiance, and whom I thanked publicly, under the belief that he had acted honestly, according to his promise to me, is the very man who advised the Pope to recognize the Southern Confederacy. My embassadors in Italy, France, and England, as well as Prof. Morse, have warned me against the plots of Jesuits. But I see no other safeguard against those murderers than to be always ready to die, as Christ advises it. We must all die, sooner or later, and it makes very little difference to me whether I die by a dagger thrust through my breast, or from an inflammation of the lungs."

Then taking his bible, the President opened it and read from Deuteronomy iii :22-28, where God told Moses to go up to the top of Pisgah and behold the promised land, for he would not be allowed to pass over Jordon. "My dear Father Chiniquy," said Lincoln, "I have read these strange and beautiful words several times in the last five or six weeks, and the more I read them the more it seems to me that God has written them for me, as well as Moses."

On the 14th of April, 1865, at ten o'clock in the evening President Lincoln was assassinated by John Wilkes Booth at Ford's Theater, and at the same hour Lewis Payne attempted to murder Wm. H. Seward. Two or three hours before this occurred, a Catholic landlord at St. Joseph, Minn., told Francis A. Conwell and Horace P. Bennett that Lincoln and Seward were assassinated. The two men make affidavit of the fact, sworn to Sept. 6, and Oct. 18, 1883. Landlord Linneman, purveyor for the priests, refuses to swear, but makes a written declaration Oct. 20, 1883, duly signed, saying that he told Mr. Conwell and Mr. Bennett that "he heard this rumor in his store from people who came in and out;

but he cannot remember from whom." That lapse of memory probably saved the landlord's life. The priests of St. Joseph were cognizant of the plot to assassinate Lincoln and Seward.

Without a single exception the conspirators were Roman Catholics. It is true that Atzeroth, Payne, and Harold asked for Protestant ministers when they were to be hung, but they had been considered Catholics till then. John Wilkes Booth was a proselyte to Catholicism, and so was Atzeroth, Payne and Harold. But had their father confessors appeared with them on the scaffold that would have opened the eyes of the American people to clearly see that the assassinations of Lincoln and Seward were planned and executed by Jesuit priests. The murderers were instructed to conceal their religion. Such is the doctrine of the Catholic Church. St. Liguori says:

"It is often more to the glory of God and the good of our neighbor to conceal our religious faith, as when we live among heretics we can more easily do them good in that way; or if, by declaring our religion, we cause some disturbances, or deaths, or even the wrath of the tyrant (Liguori Theologia, ii :3).

Dr. Mudd, at whose place Booth stopped in his flight, was a Catholic, and so was Garrett, in whose barn Booth was killed.

After the murder Father Chiniquy came to Washington in disguise. He found that the influence of Rome at the Capital was almost Supreme. The only statesman who dared to face the nefarious influence of Rome was General Baker. But several other statesmen confessed that without doubt the Jesuits were at the bottom of the plot; and sometimes this would appear so clearly in evidence before the military tribunal that it was feared it could not be kept from the public. Mrs. Surratt was a Catholic, and her house was the common rendezvous of the priests. With a little more pressure on the witnesses, many of the priests would have been compromised. But the civil war was hardly over, and the Confederacy, though broken down, was still living in millions of hearts; formidable elements of discord were still existing, to which the hanging or exiling of the guilty priests would give new life. Riots upon riots would follow. It was, therefore, concluded to be the best policy to punish only those who were publicly and visibly guilty, so that the verdict might receive the approbation of all, without creating new bad feelings. And this, they said, was the policy of the late President; for there was nothing he so much feared as a war between Protestants and Catholics.

It is evident that a very elaborate plan of escape for the murderers had been arranged by the priests of Rome. The priest, Charles Boucher, swears that a few days after the murder, John Surratt was sent to him by Father Lapierre, of Montreal, that he kept him concealed in his parsonage from the end of April to the end of July; that then he took him back to Lapierre, who kept him secreted in his own father's house, under the very shadow of the palace of Bishop Bourbet, where he remained until September; that thence he was taken in disguise by himself and Lapierre to Quebec. It further appears that he was taken from Quebec to an ocean steamer Sept. 15, by Lapierre, who introduced him as McCarty. And who was Lapierre? The canon and confidential servant of Bishop Bourbet, of Montreal. Lapierre and Boucher, who accompanied Suratt in the carriage, were the ambassadors and representatives of the Pope. Surratt was sent to Rome, where he enlisted as a Zouave under the name of Watson. Our Government found him out, and the Pope was forced to give him up. But in doing so the Jesuits managed to have him escape to Egypt. There he was arrested, extradicted, brought to Washington, and tried. But two or three of the jurymen were Catholics, who had been taught that the killing of a heretic is no murder. The jury disagreed, and the Government was forced to let the murderer go free.

The above account of the murder of Abraham Lincoln is only an abridgement from Father Chiniquy's "Fifty years in the Church of Rome," 30th edition, 832 pages, published in Chicago, by Adam Craig. Chiniquy, now in his 81st year, is lecturing in various cities. He claims to have made 35,000 converts from Romanism to Protestantism."

Henry Kidder was at one time superintendent of public schools in New York City. He had labored in the interests of its schools for twenty years and had written text-books for schools that were recognized in the French Academy. But when he wrote a book upon the subject of Spiritualism this fact gave the priesthood an excuse to dethrone this efficient man from his honored position for the reason that Catholicism exclaims that "no man has a right to think, only in the line of the Catholic faith."

Another instance of a teacher losing her position on the account of opinion, was by the treachery of a Catholic and a Protestant. Her great crime was that she believed in the immortality of the soul, based upon facts and not on faith. She conscientiously believed it was unjust for teachers to teach their belief in public schools, for the parents of the scholars are liberals, Jews, Catholics and of many different denominations, which is decidedly dishonest to take advantage of the parents' wishes at any time or at any place.

Her school was on the mountain side but the voice at the Vatican telephones by way of the confessional, the doom of the public school, all over this lovely land.

Not long ago, a small cloud was seen in the horizon of

the religious firmament, in St. Louis, in respect to the school question. In the controversy among the priests, a discovery was made that there is justice and honor some cherish for our land, and a schism was about to burst forth which would separate many Catholics from the mother Church. Some one crosses the ocean invested with his credentials of the power of a Pope and the cloud suddenly disappears, by the magic wand of his authority. This great Satolli has control over the minds of his subjects, wonderful in its effectiveness.

Catholics have persecuted the Protestants and the Protestants have persecuted the Catholics. In the union of Church and State rested the dove of peace and good-will to men, when it was the penalty of death for a Catholic priest to land on the puritanical shore of New England !

The Catholics arrive safely upon Freedom's soil and are never persecuted ! Why not learn from bitter experience the power and glory of the rule of rules, the golden rule !

The Jews land here and are among our best citizens. They are thankful to find a home of peace for their weary feet. There is no necessity of a secret organization to protect liberty from our neighbors, the Jews. The voice of Rabbi Cranskopf, D. D., is the voice of the whole Jewish fraternity :

"Religion is again clamoring for worldly power. It is forgetting that its mission is simply to support the hand of the State, by a scrupulous attending to its own duties, and not to meddle with the State in the exercise of its functions.

"Religion has grown tired of being simply the co-

adjutor to the State.   It is striving for the supremacy,
and that spirit is inimical to civilization.

"Ask for the date of that age when a deep black cloud
of appalling ignorance rested over the people; when the
intellect lay fettered; when the industries were para-
lized; when the word 'liberty' was not to be found in
the vocabulary of the people; when the physical
sciences were persecuted as being incompatible with revealed truth; when all researches were prohibited,
under the severest punishment, as being pernicious to
piety; when the grossest superstitions were forced upon
the people; when blind credulity and unquestioning belief were made the first articles of their creed; when the
most repulsive corruptions prevailed even within the
Church itself; when even the clergy was void of every
sting of conscience, drunken, rioting in open immorality,
trafficking with religion for the purpose of enlarging
their opportunities for debauchery—and the answer will
be, all this prevailed during the age in which religion
was the sole mistress of the people."

The Quakers always speak for liberty of the oppressed, but their olive branch has been rudely torn to
pieces by the union of Church and State.   Here is the
testimony of one of the descendants of the kind and loving Puritans:

THE PASTORAL LETTER.

So, this is all; the utmost reach
    Of priestly power the mind to fetter:
When laymen think, when women preach,
    A war of words, a "pastoral letter."
Now, shame upon ye, parish popes!
    Was it thus with those, your predecessors,
Who sealed with racks, and fire, and ropes,
    Their loving kindness to transgressors?

A "pastoral letter," grave and dull;
    Alas! in hoof, and horns, and features,

How different is your Brookfield bull
  From him who bellows from St. Peter's!
Your pastoral rights and power from harm,
  Think ye, can words alone preserve them?
Your wiser fathers taught the arm
  And sword of temporal power to serve them.

Oh glorious days, when Church and State
  Were wedded by your spiritual fathers,
And on submissive shoulders sate
  Your Wilsons and your Cotton Mathers!
No vile "itinerant" then could mar
  The beauty of your tranquil Zion,
But at the peril of the scar
  Of hangman's whip and branding iron.

Then wholesome laws relieved the church
  Of heretic and mischief-maker,
And priest and bailiff joined in search,
  By turns, of Papist, witch and Quaker!
The stocks were at each Church's door,
  The gallows stood on Boston Common!
A Papist's ears the pillory bore,
  The gallow's-rope a Quaker woman!

Your fathers dealt not as ye deal,
  With "non-professing," frantic teachers;
They bored the tongue with red-hot steel,
  And flayed the backs of "female preachers."
Old Newbury, had her fields a tongue,
  And Salem's streets could tell their story,
Of fainting women dragged along,
  Gashed by the whip, accursed and gory!

And will ye ask me, why this taunt
  Of memories sacred from the scorner?
And why with reckless hand I plant
  A nettle on the graves ye honor?
Not to reproach New England's dead,

This record from the past I summon,
   Of manhood to the scaffold led,
     And suffering and heroic woman.

No! for yourselves alone I turn
   The pages of intolerance over,
That in their spirit, dark and stern,
   Ye haply may your own discover!
For, if ye claim the "pastoral right,"
   To silence Freedom's voice of warning,
And from your precincts shut the light
   Of Freedom's day around ye dawning;

If when an earthquake voice of power,
   And signs in earth and heaven are showing
That forth, in the appointed hour,
   The Spirit of the Lord is going!
And, with that Spirit, Freedom's light
   On kindred tongue, and people breaking,
Whose slumbering millions, at the sight
   In glory and in strength are waking!

When for the sighing of the poor
   And for the needy, God hath risen,
And chains are breaking, and a door
   Is opening for the souls in prison!
If then ye would with puny hands
   Arrest the sacred work of heaven,
And bind anew the evil bands
   Which God's right arm of power hath riven—

What marvel that, in many a mind
   Those darker deeds of bigot madness
Are closely with your own combined,
   Yet "less in anger than in sadness?"
What marvel, if the people learn
   To claim the right of free opinion?
What marvel, if at times they spurn
   The *ancient yoke* of your dominion?

A glorious remnant linger yet,
  Whose lips are wet at Freedom's fountains,
The coming of whose welcome feet
  Is beautiful upon our mountains !
Men, who the gospel tidings bring
  Of Liberty and Love forever,
Whose joy is an abiding spring,
  Whose peace is as a gentle river !

.   .   .   .   ▬

Oh, ever may the power which led
  Their way to such a fiery trial,
And strengthened womanhood to tread
  The wine-press of such self-denial,
Be round them in an evil land,
  With wisdom and with strength from heaven,
With Miriam's voice, and Judith's hand,
  And Deborah's song for triumph given !

And what are ye, who strive with God
  Against the ark of His salvation,
Moved by the breath of prayer abroad,
  With blessings for a dying nation ?
What, but the stubble and the hay
  To perish, even as flax consuming,
With all that bars His glorious way
  Before the brightness of His coming !

And thou, sad angel, who so long
  Hast waited for the glorious token,
That earth from all her bonds of wrong
  To liberty and light has broken—
Angel of freedom ! soon to thee
  The sounding trumpet shall be given,
And over earth's full jubilee
  Shall deeper joy be felt in heaven !

                     JOHN G. WHITTIER.

CHAPTER VII.

The Clouds of Great Glory.

According to bible lore the event of Jesus making the earth a visit "in clouds of great glory" was to come to pass ere the demise of his hearers. Did they have the pleasure of receiving a call from their heavenly visitor? Certainly not. From that time down through the ages until the present period, some people are still gazing at the stars thinking Jesus will come on his mission to surprise the sinners! Nature and God are not conservative. Nature and God are no respecter of denominations. It is the chosen ones of God who are always generously disposed towards the sinners!

The Hebrews did not recognize Jesus as their deliverer, so they, too, looked for many long centuries for a Messiah. A few did appear but they involved them in terrible persecutions.

Their pretenders were overcome showing how false their claims and it is to their credit have ceased to look for impossibilities.

Messiahs appear among the Christians and they have a following. If a woman leaves husband and babies and joins the Messiah band, the Christians are not horrified for it says explicitly in the holy book about the division of families for the sake of following Jesus. The pretenders are supposed to be Jesus reincarnated and it is very moral for women to follow the modern Jesus. Christianity declares the bible teaching binds the marriage law firmly with this iron chain—"that what God has joined together let no man put asunder!" Consistency thou art, indeed, a jewel of the rarest kind!

Let us imagine the genuine Jesus has arrived, and he visits a Protestant Church and hears what the preacher has to say.

The pastor is a representative of true orthodox principles and proclaims with enthusiasm that "heresy is the worst of crimes" and the audience should shun a heretic as it would the devil and all his host.

They must be followers of the meek and lowly Jesus, if they expected to enter into the pearly gate of paradise.

The sins of this world were greatly due to the archenemy, the infidel, who is ever active in promoting disturbance and unrest in all relations of life. Beware of non-believers, for our Church is the only true Church, and keep yourselves unspotted from the world.

These remarks aroused the listener to such an extent, he arose with great dignity and informed the preacher and his fashionable audience that:

"I am Jesus, whom the Jews crucified 2000 years ago, nearly—I will inform you that I would like to be truthfully represented. In the first place, I was regarded as an infidel, by the Jewish fraternity, for trying to break their Mosaic laws, consequently, I created a sensation and unrest by the independent way I proclaimed my views. I saw cruelty exercised all around me. The Sabbath offender was beaten to death for doing little labor that was injuring no one. I also turned the rocks as they were being hurled at defenseless woman.

"My people believed they were doing right in obeying the law of God. In their ignorance they really supposed it was the inspiration directly from the great Jehovah but he had nothing to do with a creed so brutal as that manufactured by Moses. I expected my life would be sacrificed in an age of ignorance for interfering with supposed divine laws, but, walking in the line of duty to humanity, I boldly led a life that contributed to building a new Constitution of human rights that would be a better legacy to mankind than a code of blue laws that would give naught but misery and degradation.

"I was no God, neither a demi-god. I claimed repeatedly to be the Son of Man. I was a common man with the same desire, that my people should break away from a dark creed, that actuated Voltaire, Thomas Paine, and Martin Luther.

"Remember that Moses was jealous of the gods of stone and wood and he, too, wished to keep his subjects 'unspotted from the world.' All denominations are surrounded with a jealous ring for fear they will come in contact with a new idea or that a little money will go into some other Levites exchequer.

"Moses did wrong to claim that God was jealous for that is considered a very low attribute for a mortal to possess and how much it degrades the standard of an infinite being.

"I was a wizard according to the Mosaic ragime. Moses was jealous of witchcraft. Why? For the same reason that the priesthood in your time are jealous of the money paid for value received at the shrine where angels love to visit. I, too, when on earth was very near the golden gate between the two worlds, hence, my courage to dare and do for the right, and to perform the divine act of healing, etc., etc. There have been laws in the United States instituted to suppress those divinely arrayed with the gift of healing, speaking, etc., who were endowed as I to establish this natural, beautiful belief for the good of humanity.

"Changing the subject, I see you still have the poor with you. You have despised the Jews and cruelly persecuted them but they possess humanity sufficient to shelter their poor with the arms of love. They do not rest heavily upon the State. Although they have done what you consider the cruel deed of murdering a God, yet their standard is high in respect to morals. They have occupied grand positions in the different nations, and their genius in various professions have risen proudly in the annals of fame. You cannot obliterate their talents by persecution.

"Remember this, that the status of morals is lowered whenever a denomination undertakes to crush another by the cruel rocks of unkindness. Remember this, also, that when a denomination ceases to do wrong, that it will rise to become an example for the world to follow in its glorified footsteps. Remember this with the memory that is as eternal as the hills, that individuals and nations can be moral without believing that I am a God!"

Notwithstanding he was so modest in his claims the millionaires in the congregation became aware that the great reformer was a mind reader. Said he :

"What is the object that so many wealthy people attend Church? It is policy, for under the cover of respectability the hypocrite can further grind the poor with greater facility and respectability will uphold him in his criminal deeds.

"If every one that wrought crimes on the high way and byways of life that should be in the penitentiary, society would be less in number than it is at present. The reformer can find plenty to do in deflecting the rocks of the refinement of cruelty in the nineteenth century, as I, in my missionary labors in the period of my life. If there had been no crime in high life you would not hear the rumbling of the volcano of discontent at the great injustice doled out to the poor. If the law and the Church were friends to the poor, then they would be comparatively happy though not having wealth at their command.

"If the millionaires that had become rich by way of fraud were suddenly poor, lacking money to buy the actual necessities of life most of the time for one winter, would be a lesson they would not forget so long as they lived. When such men do arrive in the land of souls, they experience all the bitterness they have given to others by the most excruciating mental pain until they have expatiated their crimes which were contracted on the plane of earth life.

"I would not advise the rich to sell all their property and give to the needy but it is the duty of all mortals to be just with whom they deal.

"Aristocracy would be more humane if it allowed the still, small voice of conscience to sway its actions and to be humble for it is only through the door of humility, to resist temptation and do unto others as you would like them do unto you, will be the golden gate through which it will pass into perfect happiness and no other.

"Do not think you can escape the penalty of your sins by suddenly believing that I died on the cross as an atonement for the sins of mankind! Do not imagine my arms are filled with criminals fresh from the scaffold. They have to undergo a course of training and gradually they arise from their shadowy condition to the light of happiness.

"In respect to missionary work to foreign lands, you are merely giving the pagans their superstition but clothed with a difference in names. They have this advantage over the Christians in point of better morals, hence, it is seldom your propaganda labors meet with success. .

"My sayings in the bible are greatly magnified by priestly interpolations and this is one in St. Mark, last chapter.

"'These signs shall follow them that believe: In my name they shall take up serpents; and if they drink any deadly thing it shall not hurt them:' etc.

"Is there a missionary willing to try the experiment of handling a viper? Is there one that would drink poison to see if he had faith sufficient to withstand the poison from overcoming him by death?

"It is recorded that St. Paul could perform this trial successfully among the barbarians: When he boldly proclaimed his failing of prevaricating his word cannot be relied upon. It is wiser to be truthful at all times for it is hurtful to the priesthood and the Churches whenever they are sustained by the decayed pillars of falsehood.

"Baron Hirsh, the philanthropist, presents the finest kind of an example for Christians 'to go thou and do likewise.' Instead of spending his money to reform the heathen he gave $12,500,000 for the benefit of the Jews who were flying over the borders of Christian Russia as fugitives, and his money was given, also, to educate the children that they might become good citizens of the State.

"The Khedive of Egypt received a present of thirteen thousand pounds sterling for the purpose of erecting a monument for himself. What did he do with his money? Christians would have taken it for a sectarian purpose but this mussulman had a public school house built for all nationalities in Alexandria.

"Do not imagine that I have any use for money. Clothe the children that they may attend public schools but do not invest their minds with wild ideas of the great hereafter and above all do not threaten that a yawning hades awaits the wrong doer, for they can be won by the wand of love in doing right better than by way of fear.

"A father would not be respected if he should travel from city to city and give money to other children rather than his own. You are doing more in the cause of a divine life by giving your money to the poor waifs at home.

"What has superstition wrought for the children of the forest? It has inflamed their minds with false ideas and the Messiahs are ready to scalp their instructors.

"It is the same spirit that is incorporated in the hearts

of the pale-face brethren when the religious wars for
supremacy has raged with relentless fury on the stage of
life.   There is plenty of missionary work to be done here
in the United States, that crime may be lessened and
the reputation of the morals be upon a higher standard.
The pagan world have but little respect for Christian
America."

He glanced over the congregation and then resumed
his remarks :

"The knickerbockers, a few generations back, derived
their 'blue blood' by toiling and earning their bread by
'the sweat of their brow.'

"To ape aristocratic nobility is deplorable.   The children are taught to despise the poor, which is one source
of creating an army of tyrants.

"It is also deplorable to witness the various routes
the people take to reach heaven.   Bible scenes are re-en-
acted to attain the goal by superstition.   The missionaries make capital the way the heathen perform sacrifices
but when children are sacrificed on their altar in their
own country their voices are hushed.   What !   Is that
kind of religion the golden rule?   Did I practice aught
that was impossible?   Christians give me the credit of
raising the dead.   When you study what you think you
believe for your own spiritual benefit, you will learn that
I never claimed so monstrous a deed.   I never descended
into the hell the Christians speak about for the education
of their hearers, for the reason there is no hades only a
sensible hell of mind.

"Another false idea, I never was reincarnated.   Evolution travels onward, in the grand scale of being and
has no time to look backward, but climbs majestically up
the ladder of progression.

"Messiahs or any denomination that preaches 'entire
sanctification,' while you inhabit the house of clay is
impossible, although you can control yourselves, to a
great extent.

"It is impossible for any 'Messiah' to personate me.

Each one has a separate identity peculiar to themselves

"I have said before that I had no use for money. If my memory serves me correctly, I never erected Cathedrals, Churches, neither a school for sectarian purposes. I wasted no time in schemes to subjugate people by the sword.

"My advice to you at the present time is, to keep yourselves unspotted from ignorance, do not throw the microscope upon the floor, as the learned Brahman, for fear that science would supercede superstition.

"The Brahmin priest knew that little instrument would shake the faith of his followers in the belief of re-incarnation if they were allowed to look into a drop of water and see the different forms of animalcule life swimming in the crystal lake. It is wonderful how many millions of souls were swallowed in the life-time of only one person.

"It is wise to acknowledge that a tenent is false when it is demonstrated to a certainty that it is an error. The priesthood had better eat the food of honesty than to earn it by helping to rear a Church that is fraud from foundation to steeple. Dare to do right, though you are expelled from the bigoted ring of ecclesiasticism. Remember that the mind of the bigot contracts in the light, like the pupil of the eye, but do not be afraid to be an heretic, if need be. Advanced preachers are not all arraigned before the bar of ecclesiastical injustice which indicate that the congregations are, also, progressive.

"St. John says in the last chapter and last verse, that if all my deeds were recorded this world was not large enough to contain all the books! Verily truth is stranger than fiction!

"Reason is a bright light, and when the Churches are illuminated with its electric glow, it will be a great b.essing to mankind."

Jesus changed the current of his remarks by saying:

"That there was a great amount of insincerity among

preachers. If the pastor in the pulpit was sincere, his neck-tie would remain white, if not, it would soon change to black."

All eyes were observing the neck-tie. The preacher, somewhat amazed, had to receive the searching gaze of the congregation. The neck-tie remained white.

Jesus then said that the faces of the audience would turn black—all those that were unkind to servants or crushed the poor in any way.

Slowly and surely their faces began to change color and each one became blue and from blue to purple and they arose and went out of the doors without ceremony!

The next visit Jesus made was at the Court of Leo XIII. The Vatican seemed like the palace of a king. Valets, privy chamberlains, chamberlains, extra, honorary chamberlains, supernumerary chamberlains, house prelates, officers of the Noble Guard guardsmen, officers of the Swiss Guard and Palace Guard, foreign honorary chaplains, honorary chaplains, private secretaries, stewards and masters of the horse, many door-keepers greeted him, one thousand one hundred and sixty persons, who told him they were servants merely in this court where resided the Vicar of Christ, the follower of the meek and lowly Jesus!

At last Jesus was ushered into the room where sat Leo XIII upon his throne, surrounded with many Cardinals. Leo ordered his visitor to kneel. Jesus, perfectly self-poised, replied "that he would not crawl to any potentate, neither would he crush a woman."

Leo thought his visitor somewhat singular and told him he desired every plebeian to kneel before him as a salutation. Jesus said:

"I am a plebeian, born of humble parentage, first saw daylight in a manger, and am proud to inform you that I am a plebeian."

Said he, with the bearing of a prince:

"The golden flood of divinity flows majestically through the veins of the plebeian from Homer to Shakespeare from Shakespeare to the present. Its matchless splendor transcends the crown of kings in a halo that is most dazzling to the vision of the inner sense, the spirit."

Leo's triple crown began to sway back and forth and he readjusted it as well as he could and Jesus proceeded with his remarks:

"You have declared the divinity of kings, and that Republics cannot stand. I see thrones vanish until only twenty-seven monarchies adorn your earth and Republics increasing in number to twenty-six. Where is your infallibility in declaring so great a libel upon the scales of Justice. ? You intend to throttle the goddess of liberty by your Brothers of Good Will—the Thugs of your spiritual dominion—the Jesuits. Every land that has been ruled by the Holy Roman Catholic Pope is endeavoring to throw off the yoke and become free.

„ America is young and having had no experience, you are scheming to rule that glorious Republic. Your iron footprints can be traced upon the soil of different countries for them to read its import. It is a home for the oppressed from any nation, but not a refuge for traitors."

Leo became enraged and with the greatest disdain replied that:

"I am working for the spiritual benefit of mankind and whatever course was pursued it was the supreme desire of mine to save souls from endless perdition!"

Jesus asked his reverence, "What was the course he pursued to save souls?" "I believe in being kind to the Catholics and to the poor! I also believe in influencing the mind of children to the doctrines of our holy church before their reasoning faculties are developed which is laudable in the estimation of Jesus and the Holy Virgin !"

Jesus wished to know how it was there were so many illiterate children and poor people among his subjects when the Jews were well provided for and no poor among them ?

"What is your standing in Ireland ? How is it that many have broken away from your dominion within the past few years ? You demand your revenue when the poor are starving. You look on them with no pity and sympathize with the oppressor. Some of them are beginning to see how you love the poor. The more intelligent Catholics in America are sending their children to the public schools where their education is thorough and not superficial. In the long reign of the Popes in the world, ignorance and superstition has been like weeds run wild, and obscured the beautiful flowers of affection for home and intelligence for the masses until you have a record that is black as midnight. You tried to obliterate science by the torch. The statue of Bruno is an object lesson which is a page in your history, giving its silent testimony to your disgrace and dishonor. Science would stand in the way of Church power. Ignorance would be the pillars to prop up the flimsy structure. Science is the Sampson that will overthrow completely your dynasty. I am Jesus, the lowly Nazarene, the Infidel Jew, who, for being a friend to the poor, was crucified some two thousand years ago upon the cross and have come to make you a call in your lovely apartments for the reason you are a lover of humanity and you spend your money so advantageously where it will do the most good !"

The Pope was enraged and he wished his guards to expel the impostor. At that moment a slight earthquake shook the massive building. The Pope and Cardinals were superstitious and believed they had some sins to account for, and began to think of the Great Con-

fessional where all masks were worthless and no partiality
shown to pomp and power. The pictures swayed back and
forth, the statues and books were displaced and the triple
crown rolled to the floor. The costly gems rolled here
and there as though rejoicing in their liberty, and the
Pope lay in a swoon on the vibrating throne.

Jesus soon stood by the statue of Bruno.

"I have pity for you, Bruno," said Jesus, "for I know
what it is to suffer excruciating pain by those making
the greatest professions of piety! The humble and the
pure in heart shall be exalted when they arrive on the
crystalline shore, but the ones that have taken life in the
name of divinity will not be exempt from the penalty
of suffering for their sins and expatiating their crimes
by repentance and good deeds. By the divine law of
love and justice they return to earth in clouds of great
glory and impress mankind with their celestial ideas and
are gradually raising the darkness of sin from earth that
it may vanish in the sunlight of truth and good will
one toward another in home life, in society, in the Church
and in the State."

CHAPTER VIII.

Prayer.

The fanatics in all ages are aggressive. When reason
holds the balance of power in the mind then no faculty
runs riot out of its proper orbit and mankind is safe.

The dogmas of fear and a full faith in the efficacy of
prayer have been taught with its telling influence upon
the unthinking world.

Preachers understand that reason must be lulled to
sleep by singing, speaking of death-bed scenes and
prayer ere they can fasten ecclesiastical chains upon

their victims. The pastors reveal the fact that children and young people under thirty years of age are easily caught but not the case with those who have arrived at maturer years. Why is this? They know that reason is undeveloped. At every station on life's highway they set a trap to ensnare the unwary which must be regarded in the light of injustice and very much like dishonesty. The young devotee is prepared to believe that by faith saloons can be annihilated by lightning and the Churches will be exempt from the wrath of God. But is this the fact? Churches are often struck by lightning, and seldom, if ever, is the saloon visited by divine vengeance. Nature's laws are inexorable and do not respect the desires of any mortal. Earthquakes engulf the Church that is filled with Christians beseeching God to be merciful, and save them from death.

Exaggerated faith cannot always exist against such fearful odds. A revulsion of sentiment must be the result, disgust follows and the Church member bids farewell to the Church forever. This is demonstrated in the long poem "Lost—a Woman's Faith." The following lines are excerpts showing how grievous is the fall of faith:

"When the waters rose fast in our cottage,
    Trusting God, I crushed down my alarm,
Thinking He who'd grieve o'er a sparrow,
    Would save trusting mortals from harm.
But the water rose faster and higher,
    The little ones screamed in their fear;
How I prayed to God in my anguish,
    But, ah! there was no God to hear.

"There was nothing could swerve or turn me
    From my faith in my mother's belief,

'Twas my joy in the hours of rejoicing,
  My 'solace and refuge in grief.'
When doubts uninvited would enter,
  Their challenge, I firmly withstood,
But they conquered then, and forever,
  The day of the Johnstown flood."

Prayer may be carried so far in the domain of enthusiasm that it is not in accordance with good manners. To
call another a "sinner" is a breach in the divine law of
justice that is truly appalling. Fear of an angry God
and endless punishment obliterates any delinquency about
Church etiquette. Mrs. Livermore addressed the men
in prison as "brothers". Tears of gratitude were shed,
showing the germ of divinity sparkles in every soul.

Prayers are answered many times when it is in the
line of natural law. When a human being is suffering
for food, fuel or clothing, the appeal for assistance
reaches the conscious personality of some angel friend,
or friends, and they influence some one to help the
needy. This is certainly better employment than to be
gazing at the great Jehovah through eternity, playing
on harps and praising his holiness!

Prof. Le Conte says :

"At the bottom of every man's heart is an indistinct,
indistinguishable belief in a supreme something which is
ever present and never over shadowed. All the various
forms of nature to which we apply various names is
God. They are but divine activity. Gravitation is but
one of the forces of God, and evolution is but the divine
power of constant creation."

To force a child to pray and to tell it to go through
that form of worship or the devil will catch it, cann t
possibly do the child any good, and, furthermore, fear is

hurtful to the child, physically. It poisons the blood and it is simply a crime, for, sometimes, it ends in death by way of long illness, and again, in a very short time. Animals have been known to die very suddenly by fear alone. Again, it was reported in the "Chronicle" that fear drives people to hopeless insanity, as in the case of a young lady who recently went insane by believing that the devil was in the house and she constantly chased her imaginary foe until they committed her to the Agnew's Insane Asylum. Her name is Mary L. Garcia, aged 22 years and had resided with her mother at Niles.

When Jesus took the child in his arms, he blessed it and said the loving words, "For of such are the kingdom of heaven." He said nothing about baptism or what denomination the child's parents believed in.

The preachers preach that the Insane Asylums contain many demented Spiritualists. In being unjust to others uncovers the fact that the papers do not have the opportunity very often of giving to their readers that kind of news. How often do the items appear, however, of religious insanity. Here is a few lines that gives the unthinking Church members a true view of the case. It is:

Dr. E. W. Saunders said:

"I have had brought to my attention for treatment or consultation three well defined case of 'religious mania.'"

Further on he says:

"It is a warning of danger, nothing more, nothing less. So far as I can judge, Mrs. Woodworth is possessed of hypnotic or mesmeric powers. Emotional people are swept swiftly into the whirl of excitement and surrender to an excess of religious zeal. The madhouse awaits them assuredly if they are not dragged from the fatal influence."

Another item is that :

"Miss Arthusa Waller, 2243 Penn street, Kansas City, hopelessly insane."

In this case Sam Jones is the preacher. It would be wise that missionary money be used for keeping the religiously insane.

Religion creates aberration of mind while under undue excitement. Obsession sometimes occurs in such cases and in bible times the unwise spirit was called devil and sometimes spirit.

Jesus had the power to exorcise the unwelcome visitor. The same power is with us to-day and the healers understanding the mysteries of the occult, a natural law simply, reason with the spirit, and bidding it kindly to arise from its cloudy, mental condition, sets the insane free from its unseen oppressor.

Jesus was very much opposed to prayer in public. It was too sacred a moment to him to make a display of false sanctity before the public. He always went into seclusion, thereby he became susceptible to divine influences, for his sincerity placed him higher in the scale of being, and through the gateway of humility he became exalted.

If Jesus was here at the present time, and should be successful in getting a position as Chaplain in one of our Legislatures, he, being somewhat practical, would waste no time in advising Deity that his duty consisted in blessing the government officials, but would astonish the politicians by unfolding their many shortcomings. He would say :

"Your names appearing under the head of 'Fraud' in

the newspapers, was a disgrace to any nation that professed to be my followers."

The invocations rendered by advanced preachers and some liberals, picture Infinity with the highest attributes of perfection. They strive, by right living, to be worthy of receiving more light and wisdom that they may arrive at a conscious Nirvana of rest and peace which is obtained by practicing the golden rule in all earthly transactions. This is the way to enter into the pearly gate of The Garden of Eden where the flowers bloom forever in the soul when love is cherished for that which is divine, pure and holy.

CHAPTER IX.

Temperance.

Numbers xxviii :7, states: "And the drink offering thereof shall be the one-fourth part of an hin for the one lamb: in the holy place shalt thou cause the strong wine to be poured unto the Lord for a drink offering."

The question arises who drank the offering of wine? It must be strong wine. No lecture against stimulants here from the Great Jehovah. Undoubtedly the priests and Moses enjoyed the treat behind the scenes!

Did Jesus preach in favor of the temperance cause? Did he have numerous followers to petition the government to enact prohibition laws in regard to having a chance to persecute people which would be followed by other laws to annoy innocent individuals for the sake of a difference of opinion? Here is a verse—Jeremiah xiii :14,

"Thou shalt say unto them, Thus saith the Lord, Behold, I will fill all the inhabitants of this land, even the kings that sit upon David's throne, and the priests, and the prophets, and all the inhabitants of Jerusalem, with drunkenness !"

No pagan was ever known to leave an influence like that verse for the good of the race.

Saloons are with us. They seem as permanent as the hills. Saloon-keepers are not necessarily bad men. So long as the liquor traffic is a lucrative business they will flourish in the heart of civilization.

Experience has taught the nation that high license is to be preferred to prohibition.

Saloons are necessary for the tax-payer to economize his expenditures so the saloons can flourish. The temperate, industrious people can well afford to go without little extra comforts of life so that they may enjoy the opportunity of paying the expenses of the criminal courts accruing from first-class carousals by drunkenness. Taxes to pay for Drunkards' Homes and Orphan Asylums, destitute families, etc., etc., are paid cheerfully that the saloons may ornament the streets of every city and town of this civilized nation ! When the tax-payers positively refuse to carry the burdens that should be borne by the saloon-keepers, then the saloon traffic could not pay expenses and they would necessarily close their doors forever. In Denmark, "it is the law that all drunken persons shall be taken to their homes in carriages provided at the expense of the publican who sold them the last glass."

Men must know, also, they are responsible for the morals of their children. It is a fearful idea to cast an evil influence over the family—a shadow that is cruel in the extreme. In Melbourne the man has protected himself behind the law; if his wife is under the influence of liquor the third time, he can separate from his marriage vows without any trouble. Why not have such a law for women also? At any rate a woman should say to her husband when he reels homeward after imbibing too much stimulants:

"Take your choice between liquor or I; I shall not have my peace destroyed, my life wrecked by your failure in doing by me as you would not like me to devastate our home by a disgusting habit."

In turning the mental telescope to other lands we find:

"The Buddhists, says George A. Shufeldt, with 300,-000,000 followers, and the Mohammedans with 250,000,-000, drunkenness is unknown. The so-called heathens of the world, forbid the use of alcoholic drinks and crush intemperance, and we Christians tolerate and legalize it. We send missionaries to these people to convert them to our religious civilization."

The "Journal of a Traveler," writes that, "The Turks are better than the Christians. Wine and spirits are forbidden in the koran, and coffee is the universal beverage."

By way of fancy's sweet medium we see two men walking in a city in the United States. They are noble specimens of the human race, which we infer by their dignified bearing and intellectual features. A crowd follows them curious to know about the august strangers. The foreigners stop before a saloon. Buddha remarks to Confucius:

"What a blot upon the page of history," pointing to the saloon. "Our worthy brother Jesus did not teach temperance, hence, this creed was more imperfect than the ones we gave for the moral guidance of the race.

"Think how our followers maintained their integrity, in this respect, through so many ages, to fall at last when dashed against the Christian creed! Let the Christians reform themselves ere they try to redeem the world called paganism.

"When the lives of the ancient avaters of the world are stripped of the robes of superstition, then the ethics that were taught will have a more exalting effect upon the human race. In passing through an earthly career there are different routes to take in respect to beliefs. If you believe that which is wrong the road is rocky and full of thorns. But when traveling in the right path everything is pleasantness and peace.

"The only universal deluge that I know aught about is the vitiated influence of poisonous superstition and that deluge was one of blood and tears. That same superstition would like to make a tiger's paw of temperance to use the law as an instrument to again further its schemes in tyranny. Why not imprison every human being for fear they would commit murder? Teach the young to rise in the dignity of manhood and womanhood's estate and they will become like the Himalaya in grandeur and sublimity of spirit."

A Chinaman recognizing Confucius, prostrated himself upon the side walk in adoration of the great reformer. Confucius said to the Chinaman:

"Arise, my son, I am no God to worship. Every nation" said he, "has had one or more avaters who were of the earth earthy, but wished to give to humanity a standard of morals that would help build character for the advancement of mankind.

"The rust of superstition has dimmed the brilliancy of the golden rule, but within the next century the light of this divine creed will dispel the shadow of superstition—where hatred now exists love will take its place."

As Confucius ceased speaking, Buddha looked toward a public school house; said he:

"We taught that ignorance was the night of the mind.

We both taught the importance of knowledge in all its avenues through the groves of intellect. We would like to see its beneficent branches extend, like the banyan tree, and shelter the multitude of earth. It is knowledge and morals that are the true redeemers of man. kind. They are your saviors from ignorance and crime The emblem of liberty floating so grandly upon the temple of knowledge has more than one signification. It is a symbol of love of home by being temperate in all things, and then you are better citizens of the State."

CHAPTER X.

Tobacco.

Is tobacco a necessity? Is it a healthy or cleanly habit Does its use give an influence for good? Does it help the young to get employment? Does it give happiness or annoyance to others? Is it a sign of a very high civilization? Is it a success financially to invest in tobacco or cigars?

A LITTLE LOGIC.

"Father, do you remember that mother asked for two dollars this morning?"

"Yes, my child; what of it?"

"Do you remember that mother didn't get the two dollars?"

"Yes, and I remember what little girls don't think about."

"What's that, father?"

"I remember that we are not rich. But you are in a brown study; what is my darling thinking about?"

"I am thinking how much a cigar costs."

"Why, it costs ten cents; not two dollars by a long shot."

"But ten cents three times a day is thirty cents."

"That's as true as the multiplication table."

"And there are seven days in a week? And seven times thirty cents are two hundred and ten cen s?"

"Hold on! I'll surrender. Here, take the two dollars to your mother and tell her I'll do without cigars for a week."

"Thank you, father; but if you would only say a year—it would save more than a hundred dollars. We would have shoes and dresses, and mother a nice bonnet, and lots of things."

"Well, to make a little girl happy, I will say a year."

"Oh! that will be so nice; but wouldn't it be about as easy to say always?"

And the father said, "Daughter, I will do as you say."—[The Old Homestead.

CHAPTER XI.

Symbols.

In the first part of this book, chapter forty-third, the symbols were previously given in a lecture by Mrs. Cora L. V. Richmond, before a Children's Progressive Lyceum in Chicago, March 3rd, 1879. The symbolical language is a beautiful way to instruct people of all ages. Symbols are received clairvoyantly, which prove a great blessing in many ways. They can be impressed upon the mind while sleeping, as the snake is given as an enemy, and that being universally recognized as a fact, then others can come to denote various events about to transpire.

Symbols tell with unerring effect the moral status of a person.

If symbols are welcomed by the recipient they prove a

great blessing in social and business life—make this "vale of tears" to gradually change into a condition of mind almost angelic while living on earth.   Yet, there are many that honestly believe that only fraud is practiced at the shrine of the new dispensation.

If fraud is used, remember all classes of society are intensely human, and when it is eliminated from every mind, then will the delicate wires, or electric lines, cease to vibrate by discordant elements—consequently, better results obtained.   A dogmatic believer seldom receives aught that is satisfactory, but an honest skeptic will be fortunate in receiving the truth that life has a continued existence and is made happy thereby.   He is neither too credulous nor too incredulous, but weighs the messages in reason's scales.

CHAPTER XII.
Eden of Glory.

Cousin says, "that nation or people are most advanced in civilization which confers the largest liberty upon woman."

Rev. J. D. Fulton would civilize the world in this fashion:

"Woman is made for man.   By her use to him she is to be measured.   Her equality with her master is not to be thought of.   It is against Scripture.   Her inferiority appears in the moral realm.   She was the first tempter, the means employed by Satan in leading astray the unwary."

The above effusion was printed in a little tract in "Harper's Magazine," July, 1869.

Another representative, a colored driver, gave his idea

of the woman question. He was asked by a gifted woman, living in Lincoln, Nebraska, to vote in favor of the
Constitutional Amendment, giving the ballot to woman.
He smiled broadly, and went off to the polls with these
words: "I'd like to, but really, I don't think women's
got the capacity!"

Can women be so very closely related to Satan, as Mr.
Fulton states, when her face is seldom seen behind the
bars in a penitentiary?

Again, a representative of the negro race should be the
last one to blockade woman's pathway to liberty when
"Uncle Tom's Cabin" paved the way to their freedom by
exposing so graphically the tragedies, grief, tears, and
shame of slavery. Two million copies sold in two years
was a gift for humanity that was of priceless value.
Then again, liberal and quaker ladies spoke upon the
rostrum for the cause of humanity and were followed by
the howling mob which revealed the ghastly fact they,
too, were slaves.

Lucretia Mott was elected as a delegate with Wendell
Phillips and others, to attend a slavery convention at
London. The men were admitted but she could not be.
The noble workers who went with her tried in vain for
the assembly to admit this eloquent pleader for human
rights. She wore her clanking chains back to America
and in 1848 the first convention was organized at
Seneca Falls, but, before its final sitting, it was transferred to Rochester. This convention was convened in
the interest of white slavery—not black, but white! It
revealed this fact in the attitude that was shown by
harsh words and epithets of the press and society. They
never ceased their labors, however, and in thirty years

after, the "Democrat and Chronicle" gave them this tribute:

"Wyoming has conferred the suffrage. Its advocates have presented their arguments in Congressional halls and legislative assemblies. They have won many conspicuous publicists to their cause, and for the years they have spent in the work they have made remarkable progress. The principle of this political agitation is the one so dear to the revolutionary fathers—'No taxation without representation.' There is justness in the plea, and fortified in the assurance that they are right they will not lay down their arms until the banner is securely planted upon the last bulwark of popular prejudice.

"As a matter of fact there has been a wonderful quickening of public thought on the. woman's rights movement, and the direct and the indirect effects of that agitation, whether graven in legislative enactments or assimulated by progressive society, all must concede are of permanent value and beneficent potency. To Miss Susan B. Anthony, whose singular executive tact has turned many a dark hour into day; to Mrs. Elizabeth Cady Stanton, whose judicial skill, fine legal discrimination and splendid rhetoric has held the movement in its proper orbit, and to Lucretia Mott, whose unquenchable fervency has never known despair in defeat—to these three earnest, heroic women, the cause is indebted to a degree which can scarcely be over-estimated."

It was the eloquence of two women as speakers who helped to lift the republican party into power. One was a descendant of the quakers, Miss Anna Dickenson, and Mrs. Hardings Brittian, a liberal. Their influence over the audiences were more powerful than any two men speakers in the field. Anna Dickenson went into Pennsylvania where no man dared to go. A bullet sped by her and on account of her bravery, the tumult subsided, and listened to hear what she had to say, and they gave cheer after cheer for the message she so eloquently gave for the nation's welfare. Mrs. Hardings Brittian by her masterly eloquence wherever she went was given the first position as orator.

As the mental telescope is turned in the direction of Wyoming, there stands out in bold relief an object lesson that proves the fallacy of exclaiming that woman's rights are a failure.

It is to the honor of William H. Bright, a Democrat, who instituted the woman suffrage plank in the territorial constitution of Wyoming. He was actuated upon principle alone, for his wife held a different view of the matter.

The women have not disgraced the privileges of the franchise, and holding the balance of power, no bad men can be elected. It is now a quarter of a century since Wyoming gave the ballot to woman and many testimonies from governors and prominent men concur in the wisdom of the woman's right to be a citizen of this great republic.

A clipping from the "Nevada State Journal," Jan. 13, 1894, Judge Riner of Wyoming, says:

"Equal suffrage has proved a great success by purifying politics. Politicians who are inclined to use corrupt means to accomplish a purpose have been suppressed, and only honest men can be elected to office, because as soon as the women find out that a candidate is dishonest they proceed to fight him regardless of politics. The per cent. of women who vote are as large as the men."

It is self-evident that the taxes that women pay in Wyoming does not keep corrupt men in luxury. Neither is their earnings used as bribes in blockading laws that are intended for the good of all.

Henry George writes:

"The natural right of a woman to vote is just as clear as that of man. Since she is called on to obey the laws she ought to have a voice in making them. In fact, the failure that men have made of making laws, ought to lead them to ask whether the finer intuitions of women are not as much needed in the management of public affairs as they are in the affairs of the family. The man who scorns the advice of women is anything but a wise man."

Colorado has done wisely in following the example of Wyoming. Kansas may give woman the privilege of being a citizen at the next election. The women mayors in the different cities in Kansas have proved a success in executive and financial abilities. Over fifty years ago women were completely cowed by circumstances and really thought they were a failure in regard to not having a mind capable of being cultivaed. The Mohammedan ladies have one privilege, that of going to' the cemetery every Friday (their Sunday) and talk freely with each other. A chapel is on the grounds and they go in, perhaps, to tell Allah they are pleased they have no souls to worry over ! Our grandmothers had only one source of mental culture, which was termed "gossip," if they indulged in a social chat. To converse on various themes, is, indeed, a great source of instruction for woman as well as for man.

Young girls were once a drug in the market, not knowing how to earn a living, naturally were waiting for offers of marriage and a man was as Edward Bellamy says, "like a sultan surrounded by languishing beauties."

But he states:

"In the year 2,000 no man, whether lover or husband,

may hope to win the favor of maid or wife save by desert. While the poet, justly apprehending the ideal proprieties, has always persisted in representing man at the feet of woman, woman has been, in fact, the dependent of man.

"Nationalism will justify the poet and satisfy the eternal fitness of things by bringing him to his marrow-bones in earnest. But, we may be sure that in the year 2,000 he will need no compulsion to assume that attitude."

Young ladies of the present era being more independent by the many ways for becoming self-supporting, answer questions according to an item in the "Health Journal:"

"Did she love him well enough to live in a cottage with him? Was she a good cook? Could she make her own clothes?" etc.

The young lady said that before she answered his questions, she would tell him of some negative virtues she possessed:

"She never drank, smoked or chewed; never owed a bill to a laundress or tailor; never stayed out all night playing billiards; never lounged on the street corners and ogled giddy girls; never 'stood in with the boys' for cigars and wine suppers.

"Now," said she, rising indignantly, "I am assured that you do all these things, and yet you expect all the virtues in me, while you do not possess any yourself. I can never be your wife;" and she bowed him out and left him on the door-step a wiser man.

The way to correct the divorce question is to improve the ideas of the obligations incident to a true and lasting marriage. Sensational novels have wrought their mischief when the young lady expects a devoted hero in the character of her husband. Not expecting to meet his distorted ideas in regard to the word "obey," the crash is sure to come and her beautiful ideals have faded from her heart forever.

"Words kill," said Judge Sedgwick, in his conclusions in a divorce suit, and they certainly do. There is no apparent death, but, love, perhaps, has flown and the smile covers a tear, too often, in the home that could be a heaven upon earth when the law of love and kindness is the rule. At the altar, the true hero and heroine begin when the pledges are taken to constantly fulfill during life the requirements to love and respect, each the other, the same as in courtship days.

While women have been climbing out of past conditions, into the present, wherein she has gained wonderful success, and the achievements are founded upon merit, still she will pursue her journey like the Amazons who ascend a tall hut, thickly covered with thorns from prickly pears and cacti until she reaches the top, where the laurel wreath awaits her denoting happiness and content ever after.

The future holds in store for her success, in a political way, for her eloquence will yet reverberate through the halls of justice with telling power. She will be seen in all the departments of government to the executive chair and fraud will vanish as mist before the sunlight. Hazing is unknown when young ladies are admitted in the same college with young men.

The Catholic Church is destined to change its rule in respect to the celibacy of its priesthood. The marriage relation would change their present course into one of harmony and refinement.

In the Eden of the future it will be considered a crime to utter an unkind word.

Abraham Lincoln never would have arisen to the height he did in the nation's esteem and affection if he had been indifferent to the effect of his words. He never said an unkind word to his step-mother and she loved him equally with her own son.

A college snobs who deal largely with sneers at those he thinks are beneath him socially, can never become the peer of Abraham Lincoln in honor and fame

The secret, occult power in the life consecrated to kindness, honesty and justice is embodied in a glorious atmosphere that is a light from the great Sun of Divinity.

THE ONCOMING EDEN OF GLORY.

BY (THE LATE) PROF. WILLIAM DENTON.

We travel not back for the Eden of old,
   Bright garden so famous in story,
But forward, to gain with the noble and bold,
   The oncoming Eden of Glory.

Its gates are aye open, and no cherub stands
   To guard with a flame-sword its portals:
But angelic bands are outstretching their hands
   To welcome home timorous mortals.

On low-bending trees hang ambrosial fruits
   'Mid leaves for the sick nations' healing :
And Paradise birds, breathing music like lutes,
   Are heavenly secrets revealing.

There famishing spirits, unfed by a crumb,
   Who secretly pine in their sorrow,
Shall banquet with gods in that Eden to come,
   Unhaunted by thoughts of to-morrow.

The weary soul there on the flowery bank lies ;
  Peace henceforth he claims for a mother ;
The sleep of a baby steals over his eyes
  And angels think dreams for their brother.

   *   *   *   *   *   *

There Love, like the sun, sheds his beams upon all,
  And soul-buds expand into flowers ;
Spring brightens to summer, but winter and fall
  Breathe not on its amaranth bowers.

We travel not back, then, for Eden of old,
  Bright garden so famous in story ;
But forward, to gain with the noble and bold,
  This oncoming Eden of Glory.

THE END.

www.ingramcontent.com/pod-product-compliance
Lightning Source LLC
Chambersburg PA
CBHW020617030726
47497CB00007B/2283